Elder Race

SHADOWS OF THE APT

Empire in Black and Gold

Dragonfly Falling

Blood of the Mantis

Salute the Dark

The Scarab Path

The Sea Watch

Heirs of the Blade

The Air War

War Master's Gate

Seal of the Worm

TALES OF THE APT (SHORT FICTION)

Spoils of War

A Time for Grief

For Love of Distant Shores

The Scent of Tears (editor and contributor)

ELDER RACE

RACE

ADRIAN TCHAIKOVSKY

A TOM DOHERTY ASSOCIATES BOOK

NEW YORK

ELDER RACE

Copyright © 2021 by Adrian Czajkowski

Edited by Lee Harris

Cover art by Emmanuel Shiu
Cover design by Christine Foltzer

A Tordotcom Book
Published by Tom Doherty Associates
120 Broadway
New York, NY 10271

www.tor.com

Tor® is a registered trademark of Macmillan Publishing Group, LLC.

ISBN 978-1-250-76871-1 (ebook)
ISBN 978-1-250-76872-8 (trade paperback)

First Edition: November 2021

Elder Race

Lynesse

NOBODY CLIMBED THE MOUNTAIN beyond the war-shrine. The high passes led nowhere and the footing was treacherous. An age ago this whole side of the mountain had flaked away in great shelves, and legend said a particularly hubristic city was buried beneath the debris of millennia, punished by forgotten powers for forgotten crimes. What was left was a single path zigzagging up to the high reaches through land unfit for even the most agile of grazers, and killing snow in the cold seasons. And these were not the only reasons no one climbed there.

Lynesse Fourth Daughter was excluded from that "no one." When she was a child, the grand procession of her mother's court had made its once-a-decade pilgrimage to the war-shrine, to remember the victories of her ancestors. The battles themselves had been fought far away, but there was a reason the shrine stood in that mountain's foothills. This was where the royal line had gone in desperate times, to find desperate help. And young Lyn had known *those* stories better than most, and had made a game attempt at scaling the mountain which myths and her family histories made so much of. And the retainers had chased after her as soon as people noticed she was gone, and they'd had cerkitts sniff her trail halfway up the ancient landslip before they caught up with her. That had been more trouble than she'd got into in any five other years combined. Her mother's vizier raged and denounced her, and she'd been exhibited before the whole court, ambassadors and servants and the lot, made to stand still as stones in a penitence dress and a picture hung about her neck illustrating what she'd done. Her mother's majordomo, still smarting from when she'd stolen his wig, had overseen her humiliation. And her sisters had mocked her and rolled their eyes and told one another, in her hearing, that she was an embarrassment to her noble line and what could be done with such a turbulent brat?

And her mother, in whose name all those functionaries had hauled her back for public punishment, had just watched, and Lynesse Fourth Daughter had looked into her eyes and seen . . . not even anger but sheer exasperation. Lynesse, a child with three Storm-seasons behind her and one more to go at least before anyone might consider her grown, had done a thing nobody else cared or dared to do. Disobedient, yes; irresponsible, yes; more than that, her mother's look said, *I cannot understand what would even kindle such a thought in your head.* As though Lynesse was not badly behaved but actually sick with something.

That had been two Storm-seasons past. The sting of it had faded; the memory of that ascent had not. *Which means it was worth it,* the now-grown Lynesse Fourth Daughter decided.

They had only caught her that time because she had stopped climbing. She had only stopped climbing because she'd finally seen of what was up there: the Elder Tower. She had been the first human being to lay eyes on it for a very long time.

It hadn't looked like the pictures. In the tapestries and the books, they drew it like a regular tower of brick, with windows and a door and a pointed roof, just there amongst the mountains. Some artists had even placed it on the very peak, and sometimes drawn it bigger than the actual mountain in that way they did. They drew queens the same way, with the lesser folk only coming up to their knees. Lyn had been quite old before she had even questioned the practice, so widespread was it. That had been when an artist seeking patronage had illustrated a family history, ending with a picture supposedly of Lyn's mother and offspring, a little sequence of diminishing, facially identical figures. Lyn had complained bitterly that she was already taller than Issilesse Third Daughter, and been told, *That is not the way pictures are made.* She was smaller, under the artist's hand, because she was less important. Fourth is less than Third.

She had given their tutor ulcers for half a short-season after that, insisting that four was smaller than three when made to do her sums.

The Tower of Nyrgoth Elder, last of the ancients, was built into the mountainside. It had no sign of join or masonry. Some grand magic had just excised a great deal of the stone until all that was left was the tower, jutting from the new line of the mountainside, overhanging a chasm, reaching for the sky. The day had been crystal clear when she'd gone on her unauthorised jaunt all those seasons before, and she had good eyes. The image had stayed with her ever since.

Now she was looking on it again. Quite possibly she was standing just where her younger self had halted, though her memory didn't quite preserve that much. It was evening rather than yesteryear's bright midday, but the skies remained clear. According to the few communities that lived in the foothills, the skies over the mountain were often clear even when rain came in from the sea to trouble everywhere else. If you were the greatest sorcerer in the world then you probably got to say whether or not you got rained on, she decided. Assuming Nyrgoth still dwelled in his tower, as the legends said. He was very old, after all; he had been very old a long time ago. Even if he had not died, why should he not have travelled to some other land, or some netherworld that only wizards could access, or some other fate, bespoke to the magical, that Lynesse Fourth Daughter could not even imagine?

"You're just going to stand there, then?" her companion asked. "It's me making camp again, is it?"

Lyn was aware that, yes, it was entirely her right to demand that Esha do all the camping and cooking and the rest of it, because Lyn was royalty and Esha was not. Simultaneously she had only secured Esha Free Mark's help on this journey by explicitly promising she wouldn't act the pampered ass.

"I'm sure it's my turn," she said vaguely, eyes still upwards. "Do you think he's watching us?"

Esha squinted balefully up towards the tower, but her eyes were bad at that kind of distance. The tower was just like a little toy to Lyn; likely Esha couldn't make it out at all.

"He hasn't magicked us up to his front door yet," she pointed out. "Disrespect to the princess of the blood, if you ask me. Disrespect to my aching feet, too."

"The road to the Tower of Nyrgoth Elder is long and hard because he decreed it so," Lyn recited. "That it not be trodden lightly by fools, but only by earnest heroes when the kingdom is threatened by dire sorcery."

"I would have magicked up a bell, or something, and

I'd just turn up out of nowhere when it was rung," Esha pointed out. "That way nobody would have to do all this uphill nonsense."

Esha was of the Coast-people, who fell outside Lannesite's strict reach, and maintained a tenuous independence along the sea's edge and the banks of rivers and lakes. An independence bought with cartloads of fish and defended by the general difficulty of the terrain; hard to subjugate a people who could just go into the water at a moment's notice, and then come out of it with spears and poison darts when you least wanted them to. Her skin was pale like most of her people, greenish white and heavily freckled with blue about the bridge of her nose and cheekbones. She had a hard, square chin and her straw-coloured hair had obviously been trimmed with the aid of a bowl. She was shorter than Lyn, compact of frame, wearing a wayfarer's layers of wax-cloth and weft, with a cuirass of hard scales over it all in case of trouble.

Esha was a traveller, for all her complaints about the "uphill nonsense." She was two full Storm-seasons Lyn's senior without actually seeming much older. Lyn remembered her turning up at court at random intervals with her travellers' tales and outlandish souvenirs, and only later worked out that much of Esha Free Mark's journeying had been clandestine errands for the throne. That hard-won suffix attached to her name was the

Crown's guarantee of her right to go where she wanted without exception, and there were precious few foreigners who'd earned it.

Except, as Lyn grew up, the political landscape of Lannesite had grown more intricate, locked into a series of treaties with neighbouring states and non-states, so that Esha Free Mark's anarchistic style of impromptu diplomacy had become a little embarrassing for the throne, and she had been called on less and less. One day, so said Lyn's sisters, Esha would go pick a fight with someone, cross a border somewhere, and the writ of Lannesite would not bail her out.

When Lynesse Fourth Daughter had come asking for her help with a journey where nobody went and, after, to where nobody was currently returning from, Esha had jumped at the chance.

"I think," she told Esha now, "that it is a good thing Nyrgoth Elder did not give my family a bell to ring, to summon him."

"That so?"

"I think," Lyn went on, "that if such a bell existed, I'd have rung it with all my might before my third season just to see what happened."

The next morning they decamped with the dawn, ascending a mountain pass that seemed devoid of life, no song of beast, no chirr of creeping thing. The clear sky above shifted imperceptibly from beautiful to ominous, and Lynesse felt that there was some sound, too low or high for her to hear, that was nonetheless plucking at her innards, creating brief blooms of anxiety and fret that made her want to turn around and go back down. Glancing at Esha, she saw the same worry on her companion's face.

"The Elder doesn't much want visitors, does he?" the Free Mark said. "Doubtless he is considering some matters of philosophy and does not wish to be disturbed, by man or beast. What makes you think he'll even open his door, let alone help?"

"The ancient compact still stands," was Lyn's only answer to that. She was aware that Esha probably thought it was more myth than matter, but she had grown up on the stories; they were a part of her as much as her bones and sinew. And if not now, then when?

And soon enough, through the silent, vacant land, they had come to the tower's door, which was round and had no furnishing, not handle nor bell. The utter quiet seemed greater there, in the tower's shadow, as though there was some sound the building itself was making, inaudible to the ear and yet loud enough to resound insensibly from every rock. Looking up the tower's height towards its apex, Lyn decided that those old artists had the right of it after all. The tower was greater than its mere physical dimensions. It reached all the way past the sky to the stars.

When she'd seen the tower before, all those years and Storm-seasons ago, she'd felt nothing but excitement. The thrill of the forbidden, something made physically appreciable that had previously only existed in stories and ill-proportioned illustrations. Child Lynesse had just been thrilled that she'd made it so high, seen so far. *The Tower of the Elder Sorcerer!*

Child Lynesse had also known that her mother's servants were right on her heels at that point. *Obviously,* she'd been ready to press onwards to the wizard's very door. *Obviously.* An easy thing to swear to when you were thirteen heartbeats away from some harassed functionary's hand landing on your shoulder to haul you back.

And here she was, and there were no court menials at her heels to restrain her. She was at the very portal to the sorcerer's domain, where no other had ever stood since her ancestor had come, to beg the help of magic to fight magic. Just as she now needed to fight magic. She, the princess of the blood. The one whose *duty* it was to do such impossible things. Go to the forbidden places.

Strike bargains with the unknowable.

I don't think this was a good idea. And this was a poor time to have such a thought. In Lyn's experience, that particular regret only slunk into sight *after* she'd done something her mother wouldn't approve of. To find it turn up ahead of schedule was profoundly inconvenient because it meant she couldn't just *do* and then lament in hindsight.

"Esh," she breathed, teetering perilously at the brink of a common sense decision. *Let's just go back.* Except her friend looked at her, and there was just enough of *We came all this way* in Esha's expression that Lyn reached out with the iron pommel of her knife and rapped hard on the metal of the circular door.

She had wondered if the sorcerer had servants, and what form they might take. No form at all, apparently, for a voice spoke from the air, or perhaps from the door itself. It used sounds she did not know, although the rhythm of them, and the questioning lilt at the end, told her they were words.

"A spirit," Esha said, wide-eyed. "A spirit as his doorman."

"Howe comyst vysitingen thys owetpost?" demanded the door, its tone the same but its words now halfway familiar, sounding like Lyn's tutor when she read the old, old books.

"Did it ask who we were?" Lyn was hanging on to her nerve by a thread.

Esha shrugged, her hand on her sword hilt. "Just barble-garble to me."

"Who has come to visit this outpost?" And now the words were strangely accented but fully comprehensible, as though the voice had been listening to their conversation and reminding itself how people spoke.

A moment, in which Esha's look made plain that, of the two of them, it wasn't *her* place to answer that. And there was strength to be had, in the reciting of names to an old formula. "I am Lynesse Fourth Daughter of the Royal Line of Lannesite," Lyn declared. "I call upon the ancient compact between my blood and the Elder." Because that was how you did it. The road of those words had already been trodden, so she could force herself to follow it.

A little mouth opened in the stone beside the door, round as a lamprey's. "Substantiation of your heritage is required," the door voice told them pleasantly.

"Shouldn't have mentioned blood," Esha cautioned. Lyn stared at the mouth, knowing that there was no good way forwards.

Why else did I come? The recklessness that had brought her to the door in the first place—that would have had her child-self ring the bell, if bell there had been—had put her finger in the opening. True to form, it bit her, a pinprick jab from its single tooth. She hissed and yanked her finger out, seeing a bead of the vaunted blood royal on the tip.

"Your heritage is acknowledged," the door pronounced, and then opened, separating into six segments like triangular fangs that slid into its stone frame. The hall beyond was smaller than Lyn had expected, because surely a sorcerer could make great rooms within the bounds of a tower. Apparently, such grand chambers were not for casual visitors, though.

She stepped in, Esha following reluctantly at her heels.

"Outpost, Lyn," she noted. "Outpost of what? And where's the sorcerer?"

"He's not likely to be just standing about in his own entrance hall in case of visitors," Lyn pointed out, but the invisible voice had picked up Esha's question.

"Remain here. My master is awakening."

"Sleeping till noon," Esha observed. "There's luxury for you," but everyone knew that sorcerers could sleep for many years, replenishing their powers and sending their minds out to explore magical realms beyond the understanding of mere mortals. And Nyrgoth Elder was the last of the ancient race that brought life and people across the sky to these lands. If there was any living thing in the world that could help them, it was he.

Something within the foundation of the tower groaned, deep and tormented. In the next moment Lyn changed her mind: not a living thing at all, but as though the tower contained vast moving parts only now stirring into motion.

Nyr

MY NAME IS NYR ILLIM TEVITCH, anthropologist second class of Earth's Explorer Corps. I am centuries old and light years from home.

I come to an awareness of myself in the half state between suspension and true waking. Information drip-feeds to me at a precisely calibrated rate, guaranteed comprehensible without being overwhelming. I feel my brain and systems bootstrapping themselves into functionality.

"What messages?" I query the satellites above, as soon as my cognition is complex enough to make the query. There are very few circumstances now under which the caretaker routines would wake me, but the most sought-for is contact from the Explorer Corps.

A quick scan of the contact log reveals no such message. Absurdly quick, in fact, because the log is still empty. No word from home at all, just like last time. No word received for . . .

I am awake enough, mind and body, to clench about the thought. No word for two hundred and ninety-one years, most of which I've slept through in the outpost's suspension facilities.

At first I had myself woken at regular intervals to do my job. I came out here buoyed by the great tide of enthusiasm for rediscovering the old colonies. Humanity had seeded the stars with its generation ships over the best part of a thousand years, and those colonies had been developing on their own for a thousand more, cut off from an ecologically bankrupt Earth. But when we rebuilt, returning to space on the back of improved technology our ancestors could never have dreamt of, everyone had been keen to find the colonies and see how our lost relatives had got on.

That initiative put me out here, on Sophos 4. There was a team of us, although I actually have to query the database before the names and faces of my colleagues come back to me. They left. Things were going wrong at home and I volunteered to hold the fort here, for the love of anthropology, while they headed back. It was only supposed to be a stopgap measure. But the gap grew and grew, and I had to sleep more and more to stop myself growing old in my study here.

I may also have breached various non-contamination regulations, in respect of the locals here, but then the outpost itself, while remote, isn't exactly invisible, and they came calling. And I was curious, and I was lonely, and there was nobody around to tell me to keep the rules.

I check the maintenance logs next. The outpost system self-repair is within tolerance. The suspension system itself has the most wear, and at first I assume that's why I've been woken: so it can tune up the facilities that are keeping me alive. By now my body is working and I can sit up. I am still very cold, and the outpost has a heated robe and slippers for me, fabricated and disposable, inlaid with arabesques of circuitry in fine gold against the uniform slate grey of the Explorer Corps.

The system pings me to let me know it is expecting a decision on something. I have managed to overlook the actual thing it needed me for, typically. A terribly bleak wave of depression hits me, and I can't see what the *point* of any of this is. Almost three hundred Earth years; I have been cut off from home for that long, and I don't even know why. No word, no visit, not the least transmission. The distance between stars is vast, but not enough to account for so long a silence.

I get a prompt about using my Dissociative Cognition System. It takes considerable effort to make even that decision, but I manage to give my systems the OK and immediately I can step back from the crushing burden of misery, cut off from certain aspects of my own biochemistry so that I can function and make rational decisions. It was an essential mod, for someone who was going to be on their own for long periods of time without any social contact. My emotions are still out there, and I can get fascinating readouts about what that locked-away part of me is actually feeling, good, indifferent, bad, worse, but it doesn't touch me unless I choose to open the door again. It's a fine line, I suspect, between useful logic and that pathological numbness that true depression can often lead to, where doing or wanting anything seems like climbing uphill. The DCS is well designed, though, and for now my reason is steady and engaged and the churn of my feelings prowls about its cage and lashes its tail. I set timers and reminders to let it stretch its legs later, when the worst will, I hope, have ebbed, when I can afford to indulge it.

"Report, then."

"I have admitted visitors from the subject population."

That seems like a profound flaw in outpost security, not to mention all the procedures designed to avoid non-contamination of the locals, but the outpost reminds me that this is all based on my past orders, which it is powerless to disobey. Do I sense a tone of reproach? I wouldn't be surprised.

But, yes, I did tell it that. One of my many lapses of judgment. Be alone enough, let your emotions out of the box enough, you're going to make some poor calls. And if the Corps would just come *back* for me, I'd take the rapped knuckles. But they haven't. Which, after that much time, very likely means that they won't. Ever.

I hear the great hollow vacancy where my depression should be, if it wasn't locked away. These are the thoughts that lead me down dark paths. I need to find something positive to think about, and apparently there are some locals who've come up the mountain. Perhaps they've brought offerings or gifts. Perhaps they're going to try to kill me or something. They are barbarous creatures after all. It will, in any event, be a diversion.

Before descending to the base of the outpost to meet with them, I check over the security diagnostics: more than equal to any attempt to harm me using known local technology. Of course, some of my involvement with the locals has revolved around when they got hold of old colonial-era tech, much of which remains buried about the planet wherever the original pioneers left it. The locals themselves maintain a post-tech society, but the old tech rates highly for ease-of-use, and historically those who uncover working remnants are not slow in finding ways to use perfectly innocent tools as weapons.

If these visitors have something like *that,* then the outpost systems may have to work a little harder to protect me. I examine how I feel about that. I feel nothing about it, which is precisely the downside with relying on DCS routines to shield me from my emotional responses. Theoretically I should be making better judgment calls without my animal half tugging me around in its teeth, but that same animal half is responsible for giving me my priorities. Right now I can make the decision, entirely rationally, that if the savages kill me with salvaged old Earth tech, that's just a thing that will have happened.

Descending in the elevator, I am very aware of all the sad I am not feeling, how lonely and lost I don't care that I am, and how trivial it is that I am utterly cut off from the civilization that gave rise to me, and anyone who might know or care who Nyr Illim Tevitch is. Yes, all these things are inconsequential and I don't have to feel them. I just peek into their cage and watch them looking up at me hungrily, waiting to be fed.

And then I am striding out into the base of the outpost, ready to confront the barbarian horde. But there are only two of them, two women. One of them is familiar. I stop, because I am getting a great deal of information from my locked-off emotional state, which has had a change of heart. Positive things. It hardly seems likely, but apparently I'm feeling good about something.

I disable the DCS and sip at my emotions, feeling a dizzying whirl of fondness, happy nostalgia, the onrush of memories that previously were just data and are now recalled experience. How we fought! How we rode together, where the fighting was thickest. I remember coordinating with the satellite to bring her word of her enemies' movements. I remember dusting off the equipment locker and going into battle—into *battle*, me, the anthropologist!—at her side. I could have stayed. I almost stayed with her, and grew old and died. A woman of a primitive culture who could never have understood what I am, and yet magnificent, radiant. And I had been alone for so long by then.

With my DCS hat on, it's clear that I suffered multiple lapses of professional judgment when I met her last. I should put that hat on again, to stop me suffering more of them, but I am just looking at her and remembering how good it was, to have company and not be alone for a while. Even company of a different culture, virtually a different species. It's always a shock, when I look on them the first time after waking. I forget how their stock and mine have diverged since the first colony ships left Earth. She is closer to baseline than I, but then the second great rise of Earth culture was one of grandiose ambitions and a refusal to accept limits, even the limits of human form. I am much altered from my ancestors, within and without, and these post-colonial natives have changed little.

But I stride forwards, feeling all these good things, and I remember the correct form of address.

"Astresse Regent, welcome again to my home!" No handshakes or clasped shoulders or physical contact, not yet, not casually, because I recall that as a cultural taboo—a people who save such things for when they have meaning. Just an open hand to signify peace, arms wide to signify trust.

And silence. Awkward silence. I stand there, with those wide arms, and the two women stare at me. I am again reminded how different I look from their kind: I am a head taller than either of them. And there are the horns.

I have a lot of complex instrumentation in them. They are useful augmentations to the natural human state. But I am anthropologist enough to know that Earth Resurgent adopted the modifications primarily as a display affectation, one which has in the past caused some alarm amongst the locals here.

That is not the sole reason for their being taken aback, however.

"Astresse," says Astresse slowly. "Astresse Once Regent was my great-grandmother, Nyrgoth Elder."

I stare at them. All those happy memories have lost their colour, all at once. I clutch for them, but they are like sand, gritty and abrasive. Sand under the eyelids. Sand in the mind. And of course she is dead. The outpost reported dates and times faithfully. If I had been thinking properly, I'd have been fortified against the revelation, not even have made the mistake in the first place. It has been well over a century, at least twenty-five of the locals' long years, their "Storm-seasons," as they call the dual-lunar cycle of climatic chaos that sweeps this world. Astresse, at whose side I rode to war in the most absurd and glorious venture of all my long years, has been dust for generations.

I force myself to re-establish the DCS, distancing me from the fresh wave of despair about to crash down on me. It is almost more than I can manage. Part of me just wants to give up, at that point. But seeing this girl, this stranger, gave me such hopes.

And now I am rational again, and all that nonsense is locked away, and I compose my face and look sternly at the pair of them, constructing my sentences in the local dialect, whose roots to old Earth languages I painstakingly dissected centuries before.

"Why are you here?" I ask, or at least that's the sense I'm aiming at. The locals' speech is ornate and filled with qualifiers and conditionals, so perhaps it comes out a little fancier than I intend.

Lynesse

"**FOR WHAT PURPOSE** do you disturb the Elder?"

Nyrgoth Elder was seven feet tall, gaunt, clad in slate robes that glittered with golden sigils, intricate beyond the dreams of tailors. Lyn imagined a legion of tiny imps sewing that rich quilted fabric with precious metal, every tiny convolution fierce with occult meaning. His hands were long-fingered, long-nailed; his face was long, too: high-cheekboned, narrow-eyed, the chin and cheeks rough with dark stubble. His skin was the sallow of old paper. He had horns. In the old pictures, she'd thought they were a crown he wore, but there they were, twin twisted spires that arched from his brows, curving backwards along his high forehead and into his long, swept-back hair. She would have said he was more than half monster if she hadn't known he was something half god. He was the last scion of the ancient creators who had, the stories said, placed people on the world and taught them how to live.

And now she had been silent too long. Esha jogged her elbow and she burst out, "I call upon the ancient compact between the royal line of Lannesite and the Elder, where you bound yourself to aid the kingdom should foul magic rise against it. A new threat has arisen who wields terrible powers, as did Ulmoth in the time of Astresse Once Regent. Ulmoth whom you met sorcery with sorcery and cast down."

The Elder's look at her was haughty and dismissive. There had been a moment, when she told him of Astresse, that she had thought to read human responses in those arch features, but now she looked on him and could only see the distance between them.

"I am not troubled by such small matters," he pronounced. "These disputes you must resolve yourself. It is not fit for me to intervene," and he turned to go.

Lyn had a whole speech prepared—literally memorised by heart—in which she recited the Lineage of Queens, elucidated the deeds of her great-grandmother and the legends of Nyrgoth Elder and made a formal plea, diplomat to great power, for the honouring of bargains. There was an expected language to these things, just as though one were telling a tale, conventions to abide by. One did not just charge into the tower of a sorcerer and take liberties.

And yet he was already going away, without any of her elaborate charade enacted, and she just lunged forwards and tugged his sleeve, as though she were a peddler and he was departing without paying.

The robe punished her. There was a crackle and a feeling as though it had bitten her fingers. Then she was sitting on the floor, hand ringing with pain and tears in her eyes. Esha had grabbed her shoulders and was trying to haul her back, gabbling apologies to the Elder, begging him to forgive the princess's temerity. Nyrgoth just stood there, looking down at her, seemingly as surprised as she was by the development.

At last, he said, "Forgive me. The things of this tower are jealous of me, and careful in my defence." And then, after unnamed things came and went in his eyes, "Astresse did the same, when she came to me and I told her I would not intervene."

"And you did intervene," Lyn reminded him. "Elder, there is a new power arisen in the Ordwood that men say is a demon who steals minds, whom the strongest cannot face with a blade. The forest kingdoms are falling already. Lannesite's roads are heavy with those fleeing their homes." *And my mother will do nothing,* she thought but did not say. No gain in telling the Elder that she was not exactly here with royal sanction.

"Please," she said, all those fancy words she'd learnt condensed down to that one. "I invoke the compact between us," she went on, but quietly, an entreaty and not a demand. "You promised my family, long ago. Are the vows of a sorcerer nothing?"

Nyr

MY PROFESSIONAL ASSESSMENT IS that I let myself behave in a remarkably unprofessional manner some time ago and here it is, back to bite me. True, there is a loophole in the non-contamination procedures where advanced technology is concerned. Not a terribly well-reasoned loophole, given that the tech that the warlord Ulm had got hold of wasn't ours at all, but a holdover from the colonial days. I would have been within my rights to decide that whatever he did with it was just part of the natural development of the society here, and hence that anything I did would just have been unconscionable meddling.

And yet whoever worded the contamination regs for the Corps was less than exacting, meaning that I could, if I wished, interpret them to mean that I could go and take down Ulmoth and restore the proper post-tech balance that I was supposed to be studying.

My rationalistic assessment, with Dissociative Cognition System engaged, is that I made the incorrect decision back then, and would only compound matters now.

In fact, DCS on, I literally cannot understand why I weighed in to help Astresse. I can recall our first meeting word for word, and yet the decision I made makes no sense to me. On this basis, I feel I cannot make a final decision now, because I feel I lack some nebulous information I obviously possessed then.

I put a hand out to help this new woman to her feet and she flinches back. "I have tagged you as safe for my systems here," I assure her. I have already apologised for the efficiency of the outpost's defences, which interpreted her movement as an attack. Thankfully I had them set only to warn in the first instance, or the cleaners would be sweeping up her ashes.

Looking at her expression, I suspect that my grasp of the language remains imperfect, or at least lacks nuance. On the one hand, I could write you a dissertation on the linguistic roots of their various tongues in Old Earth stock and how they have developed since this colony became cut off from the wider human diaspora. On the other, I suspect that there is a whole level of subtext hidden amongst their suffixes and registers, cases and inflections where every word has a dozen different variants depending on precisely who's talking to whom about what. I've wondered if, early on in the colony's development, the colonists sat down and decided that they really, *really* needed to be clear about exactly what everyone meant, and now the language is a tangled thicket I have to hack through with a machete.

All of which is getting me nowhere nearer to making a decision. I should just go back into suspension and have the outpost wake me when . . .

When?

And at last I identify the gap in my perfect tower of logic. DCS-mode is intended to let me make rational decisions without the short-termism of undue emotion. After all, even if things hadn't gone horribly silent back home, this was always going to be a centuries-long posting as we watched the native culture develop; long-term thinking requires a clarity the natural human mind is not good at. Except long-term thinking also requires a goal to plan towards, and that is where I find the frayed end of my tether. I have no guarantee that there will ever be word from home. Three centuries of silence says there won't be, and that I am a remnant of a culture whose second flowering into space, that seemed unstoppable and glorious, was actually just brief and doomed. I am more a relic worthy of study than those I was placed to observe.

My visitor, who so resembles Astresse, *she* has a goal. She was sent to petition me for aid against some warlord who's found and activated an old excavation machine or flier or neural pacifier or some such nonsense, and is using his toy to carve out a kingdom. And I shouldn't care, and I shouldn't interfere, but there is a great vacant void where I would normally keep all the things I *should* do. There is only one driving purpose in the room and it is not mine.

For a moment I am about to disable the DCS shielding again and let all that emotion in. My readouts suggest that I am feeling quite a complicated cocktail of things right now, and it might be interesting to actually experience that, rather than just read over the reports. I am still looking at my visitor's face, I realise, hand still out to help her up. She has frozen like a rabbit before a serpent. I force myself to straighten up and step back, because we've been like that for some time now and it's a bit awkward. Her friend or servant helps her stand up. That one's a descendant of the old kelp farmer augments, a labour division of the first-generation colonists which somehow became an inherited trait and then a whole population. I have an incomplete report on the subject that I feel I'm not going to get round to finishing. And now I'm staring at her, and she has her hand on the hilt of a weapon and obviously feels threatened. I need to stop making eye contact; it's culturally inappropriate here compared to back home. Like touch, it's not a casual thing.

"I will go with you to . . ." and I can't even remember where she said this warlord has set himself up, except it can't be that far because all the kingdoms are tiny here. "I'll take a look at whatever this is and see if it's my business." Without emotions to influence me, my decision is purely based on the fact that I made this decision in similar circumstances before. Or that is what I'll put in the report, anyway. It's possible I'm experiencing some bleeding through the DCS. It's also possible that I'm just resigned to being a very bad anthropologist. Which is a shame. I might be the last one left.

Lynesse

THEY TOOK THE HIGH passes away from the sorcerer's tower, ostensibly because, with Esha as guide, it was a swifter road to the Ordwood than winding around the foothills on the wheel-roads. She had a whole speech prepared, elaborately constructed to conceal the fact that she was, in truth, avoiding being seen by any who might carry a message back to court about what the queen's delinquent youngest daughter was about. As matters fell out, he seemed not to register that their path was unusual, and just strode along in their wake without word or comment.

There were no songs sung for a Fourth Daughter, nor did histories often record them. Certainly there were none for a Fourth Daughter with a past as chequered as Lyn's. She had met the formal adulthood of her fourth Storm-season with none of the accomplishments of a princess. She did not play music, nor could she manage the accounts of a fiefdom. Her one venture into diplomacy had been disastrous. Her sisters had quietly put aside stories, brawling and running away from their lessons. Suddenly they had all three become responsible human beings while Lynesse was still clinging to her childhood. They were all polite manners and needle wit. They'd rather the formal appreciation of the duel than stories where the enemy leader was called out to single combat. Rather ambassadors and accountants and intelligencers than foolish talk of heroes. Or sorcerers.

And the desperate petitioners who had come from the Ordwood's forest fiefdoms had hardly been ambassadors. Travellers bearing unlikely stories, refugees babbling of horrors. Lannesite merchants fleeing home with their goods unsold. And, in the midst of this rabble, a handful of emissaries from this woodland hold or that, begging aid.

A demon, they said. A thing that could not be fought. That was devouring the wood and its fiefdoms both. Evil magic that had not been seen since the days of Astresse Once Regent and her war against Ulmoth. And perhaps it was their attempts to conjure by *that* name which had sown the seeds of Lynesse's own action.

Because her mother, the queen, had heard them all out. Had sorrowed with them. Had expressed the Crown's deepest sympathies. And then, in private council with her daughters and advisers, had confirmed that nothing would be done. Nobody believed there was a demon, only that the eternal infighting between the forest polities had reached some new peak, and every finger pointed at its neighbour and cried dark magic. Not for the first time. And fighting between the Ordwood fiefdoms was, perhaps, no bad thing for Lannesite influence. Should the queen bring any force across the Barrenpike and into the trees, she'd only be miring her realm in a generation of squabbles and skirmishes.

There is no demon, was the enlightened decision of the queen and her council. *Let them sort out their own mess. We'll shed no Lannesite blood over it.*

Even when Esha had come forwards, still the court's roving eye out in the world from time to time, the queen had been unmoved. She'd listened to the woman's eyewitness accounts of the displaced host of forest dwellers camped at the banks of the river, of their second-hand tales of monsters and corruption and the uncanny run wild, and she'd dismissed it all. *No doubt they suffer,* the queen had agreed. *But there is enough in war and bad harvests without inventing a supernatural threat.*

Lyn had nodded along, but in her head were all the old stories. She'd barely been able to focus on the actual words spoken, because of the older and far more persuasive words in her mind. *Astresse Regent rode forth, and at her side the sorcerer.* Battles against Ulmoth's monsters. The undoing of evil magics and the salvation of the realm. And so she'd gone herself, after that closeted council meeting. She'd spoken with those same emissaries, heard their wild stories. She'd tried to pierce through their panic to some mundane kernel of internecine strife, just as her mother believed. But it wasn't what the refugees believed. *A demon.*

She wasn't a child anymore, and her mother and her sisters and her tutors and the snide majordomo took pains to remind her of it, until she had looked in the smudged bronze of the mirror one morning and known it was true. And that things like the glorious ballads of Astresse Regent and her sorcerer were becoming like the bright clothes she could barely fit into, where all her new clothes were severe and stateswomanlike and sombre.

And the Ordwood refugees spoke of demons, convinced of it, and it was as though Lyn heard different words to everyone else. In their ears it was just *war* and *civil strife* and *the traditional political instability of the Ordwood region* as her tutor would say. In hers it was *demons* and *dark magic.* Enemies from the stories, that only another story could defeat.

Astresse Once Regent wouldn't have sat idle, with or without her sorcerer. And so Lyn had talked herself into a position of moral righteousness in which this last reckless fling of childhood could just about be seen as upholding her family duty and honour.

The fact that bringing a sorcerer into a neighbouring

land was probably not in accordance with her mother's foreign policy had since crossed her mind, but at speed because she had actively chased it to the borders and watched until she was sure it wasn't coming back any time soon.

———————

Another thing the sorcerer didn't understand was fires. Or presumably he understood *fire*, but he didn't know what to do with it. When Lyn and Esha huddled close to the blaze against the chill mountain nights, Nyrgoth Elder just sat off by himself. She half expected to find him frozen the next morning, but there was a circle about him where the frost hadn't touched, and which was toastier than the fire's ashes by the time dawn rolled around. Not that she'd dare warming her hands on the sorcerer. He'd doffed his gold-embroidered robe for the journey, appearing in clothes that looked as though they'd been made by a blind tailor who'd had real human clothes described to him once. They were of strange materials, shiny in places, utterly lustreless in others, and mostly without visible weave or obvious buttons. He had a hood, but he was too tall and too oddly made to blend into any crowd Lyn had ever seen.

Two days later, as they were beginning their descent towards the banks of the Barrenpike, a monster attacked them.

Back in the coastal marshes that Esha called home, there were things called Stirg-wasps, many-legged flying things half the size of a man that hatched from stagnant pools and drained the fluids of people and animals. Esha's people went beating for them every other short-season, killing their slug-like aquatic larvae wherever they were found. The thing that attacked them was some-thing like one of those but ten times the size, and instead of a halo of beating wings it had two motionless discs that kept it lurchingly in the air. It had no beak; rather, its entire head was composed of whirling blades and sharp-toothed wheels. An eldritch monster, plainly, and it came for Nyrgoth with a furious whine. Esha cast darts at it that rattled from its metallic hide, but Lyn got in its way with her sword, battering it furiously across the night-mare of its face.

It chewed up her blade, ripping the weapon from her hands and shredding the fine steel, the best her mother's smiths could forge. She was left with her arms extended in a perfect warrior's form, hands empty, staring at that oncoming storm of jagged, translucent teeth.

Nyrgoth spoke a word and then three more, and the monster veered away, screaming in a voice almost too high to hear. Then he shouted after it, spitting out more arcane syllables until the demon dropped from the sky and crouched timorously on its five legs, the moving parts of its head slowing to a stop.

The sorcerer's hand fell on Lyn's shoulder and she stiffened at the uninvited touch, waiting for the magic or the curse that must surely follow, some punishment for her stupidity. Instead, he just moved her out of the way, gently but firmly, and then went to converse with the monster, leaving her feeling the nag of unfinished business, that she owed him something, or he owed her.

The monster spoke to him in reedy, piercing tones, twittering and singing like the wind over wires. Nygoth made three pronouncements, sequences of sounds that had the rhythm of sentences, each with its own termination, and none of which Lyn could make anything of. Esha was listening keenly, though; polyglot traveller as she was, perhaps some words of wizard-speak had meaning to her.

Then the demon was aloft again, just rising vertically into the air with its legs folding beneath it. It said one more thing to the wizard and then wobbled off into the air, heading for the higher peaks until it was lost to sight.

"It sensed certain talismans that I bear," Nyrgoth Elder said apologetically. "It would not have troubled you if I were not here. I have bound it with oaths and, though I fear it may yet seek me out again, it should not threaten us."

His words were portentous, and yet his manner suggested that he found the whole episode less than the stuff of legends, something soonest done and soonest forgotten, as her tutors used to say when disciplining her.

That night, the last by Esha's reckoning before they came to Wherryover and the haunts of men, he sat away from the fire again, his back to a stone and staring up at the peaks as though seeking the monster out again. Still feeling the imprint of his hand on her shoulder like an itch, Lyn approached him.

"Is it your enemy from another age, Elder," she asked formally, "the monster?"

He frowned at her blankly for a moment and then said, "It was but a worker whose masters are long dead. It wants to be of use, if only anyone needed any of the tasks it was made for. Your warlord, Ulmoth, learned command over such things from his study of the old languages." The words were slow to come from him, and he seemed oppressed by something, even if it wasn't the return of the creature.

She knelt, because it seemed disrespectful to stand and look down on him. The light of Esha's fire chased over the rocky ground and touched his face, making it seem carved from pale stone a long time ago. It caught in his beard and the ridges of his horns, his long nose and fierce brows. All of a sudden she was very aware of how human he wasn't, how everything about him was just an approximation of her kind, or perhaps all the people she ever knew were but poor copies of his.

"Forgive me, Elder. If not the monster, then there is some other foe in the world that causes you concern?" The thought was dire, and yet there was something weighing on him, and surely one did not become a great sorcerer without making great enemies.

"There is a beast that has hounded me down the centuries," Nyrgoth told her. His hand lifted, and she shivered and leant back in case he should touch her again. His words filled her with a sense of creeping dread.

"It is always at my back," he continued, "and sometimes it grows bold and its teeth are at my throat. It drags me down, and if I did not carry a shield against it, I could not get up from beneath its weight. But perhaps it is the same with you, or some of your people, though maybe they have never told you. Such beasts hunt in secrecy; even their prey are loath to speak of them for fear of showing weakness."

"My uncle was killed by a cerkitt, a wild one," she said uncertainly, but she knew it wasn't the same thing. A beast that hunted sorcerers would doubtless savage a thousand men like her uncle and barely pause. She shuddered and returned to the fire and slept very poorly.

Nyr

I WAS TRYING TO be reassuring, but I evidently failed and now I'm not entirely sure what she made of my words. She seemed so solicitous, though, and I was trying to bleed off the build-up of sentiment that the DCS was keeping at bay, just like the operating manual says you should, to avoid unhealthy hormonal build-up. You can't put it off forever, basically, but you can tap into it when circumstances allow, feel things when you have leisure to, and keep everything under control.

And so she wanted to know why I looked sad, and I explained it was basically a long-term mental state and that it was all under control, but that didn't seem to be what she heard. And of course they don't have a precise word for "clinical depression" or anything like that.

I did set her mind at ease about the mining robot, anyway. Not even an old colonial model, that one, but something left over from our own mission, gone wrong in its mechanical brain over a few centuries of inaction. And she nearly lost both hands at the elbow to it. It wasn't trying to attack us, although it would have killed her on its way to me if I hadn't had the codes to reset its priority queue.

And she stood in its way, when it was plainly going for me. Astresse would have, as well. In fact, she did, when Ulmoth sent his reprogrammed machines to destroy me. She almost died, too. We both did. But we prevailed: the white of her grin as they patched her wounds; her musician, extemporising the saga of the fight; she leant in to me and touched foreheads, her diadem rasping against the base of my horns. Meaning respect; meaning camaraderie, shared hurts and healing. Meaning intimacy. Good times. Good times three lifetimes gone, and here I still am.

And it's time I re-established the DCS, feeling the beast standing behind me, sour breath on my neck. It fades as the system shields me from myself. I know it's still there, but its teeth cannot pierce my armour.

Lynesse Fourth Daughter sleeps by their fire while Esha Free Mark keeps watch. I adjust the temperature settings of my underclothes and lie down over here on my own, feeling simultaneously noble and foolish for being so.

After another day coming down from the mountain,

stepping up our pace to make the walls before nightfall, there is a town. Progress has been brisk, and I have had to step up my metabolic augments and mute some pain and fatigue tells to keep up with the two women. However, reaching the walls of the town with some remaining spring in my step prompted a spike of positive emotion that I was able to tap off and experience. Thus avoiding my dissociative system from becoming overwhelmed.

I have seen satellite images of this place, and sent un-obtrusive drones to record the goings-on here, in the name of scholarly study. When I worked out where we were going, I thought the place would seem familiar. It's very different when you're actually there, stepping through the gates scarce moments before they're closed for the night. Meeting the stares of the locals.

When I had the outpost facilities fabricate these clothes for me I fondly imagined passing incognito amongst the locals, to keep contamination to a minimum. They were made to replicate the colours and styles of the local dress, but now I see that everything is somehow wrong. I feel like an actor in a poor historical reproduction, or some tourist who has bought cheap tourist trash from the tourist shops, and now imagines themselves very cosmopolitan and multicultural. The cut is wrong, and the way the garments hang off me is more wrong, and everything is sealed where it should fasten and vice versa. And I am a full thirty centimetres taller than anyone else here. And I have horns. I'd thought the hood would help, but my roving camera drone shows me that the very way the cowl sits shouts out their presence. In the end I just accept that anthropological training, second class, does not make me a master of disguise. I pull down the hood with something like disgust, and just let them stare. The DCS keeps my embarrassment and awkwardness at bay, and I pass through them with a neutral demeanour, as befits an academic.

Lynesse Fourth Daughter and Esha Free Mark seem to take the attention I'm getting as only right and proper. There are people they will talk to in the town, they say, or at least Esha will, and Lynesse will stay with me at some sort of hostelry. In the Landing Site territory, lodgings are not solely to be had by money or exchange of goods, or so I understand. One must have a right to sleep the night beneath a roof in this country and most neighbouring states, which right is granted vicariously by the hereditary government. I'd assumed that her royal pedigree would suffice for that, but instead it was Esha showing papers to the proprietor, a thin-faced, hollowed-out-looking man. Esha's status is interesting, and I should take the time to compile some notes, to satisfy . . . some notional future visit by anyone who cares. But with the DCS up, *I* care, or at least feel that it is something that should be done. Except the judgment calls the

DCS is supporting are themselves fundamentally irrational, holdovers from a time when there was a wider academic institution I could report to. I think about this, and my readouts say my emotional state drops immediately, my cheer gone. By then I have put the shield back up, and so the whole business just loops about in my head like a bee trying to escape, and then we are at the hostelry.

The host, some manner of minor civil servant within the highly complex hierarchy of the Landing Site state, stares at me more than anyone, and at my horns especially. He is frightened, but also wants to touch me, or at least his hands make little clutching motions when he looks at me. This is, frankly, a poor and filthy place, and I'm glad I have been thoroughly inoculated to the cocktail of microorganisms that make Sophos 4 their home—the native forms and the Earth forms and the runaway hybrids resulting from incautious engineering by the initial colonists. People on this world get sick so often that I was amazed any of them survived to their majority, during my first observations, and while they have basic procedures regarding washing and handling food, their reasons for so doing owe little to microbiology. This hostelry, which Esha calls the Armoury Gate, seems even filthier than it has any need to be, but I am doubtless imposing the standards of a higher technology unfairly. After all, Lynesse is a child of queens. This is presumably the most luxurious accommodation this town grants.

Once Esha has gone, we sit in the common room with the gawkers. I compose reports and make notes to my internal record. Lynesse fidgets and tries to avoid notice, not hard when all eyes are on me. Eventually I try to make conversation.

"When I travelled with your ancestor, it was not like this. There was an army and servants and all manner of ceremony, musicians, acrobats, tents with golden ships on them."

"I'm sorry. These are different times."

She mutters the words and I add quickly, "It doesn't matter to me. I am a scholar. I do not need armies or servants."

She looks up sharply, suspecting mendacity I think, but my face is in its neutral aspect, and she looks away abruptly. Something unkinks within her, though, and I feel I have scored a point for social anthropology. A lot of their codes here revolve around obligation, both to and from power. I have released her from feeling that she owes me something she was not providing. Hence, the moment of social awkwardness has passed, well done me. Except after that, there is just another sort of awkwardness, and I realise that I have been seeing her with my eyes, but seeing long-dead Astresse with my mind. It is not the drink I have, the toxins of which are neutralised even as I imbibe, but bleed-over from my DCS. I will have to turn the whole system off and suffer a bleakly miserable night of doubt and recrimination, I think, so that I can face tomorrow with a brittle, clear head. That is my half of the awkwardness accounted for, anyway. Her own is not so much to do with me, but the people around us and the task ahead.

"The demon who has taken the forest kingdoms and driven out their people," she says, in a low voice. "It is not like Ulmoth. No one person has come forth as the master of the monsters that steal people's will and despoil the orchards and the ponds. It is a terrible sorcery that comes on the wind and blights whatever it touches. But, because it does not come with swords or threats, all who hear of it are slow to believe it." She leaves that last word hanging, but the implication is plain.

"You are not here with the formal writ of your mother," I say. She flinches as though I had touched her and shakes her head.

"I am a scientist," I tell her, or the best fit I can using her words. "I did agree to help your family against threats like Ulmoth, because they are threats that do not arise naturally from your world or culture, and so are the business of scientists. It does not matter that we are not riding in at the head of your mother's army."

I suspect that I have phrased the whole concept

poorly, but in that moment I don't care because she gives me such a smile, and I realise that she had been dreading breaking this to me. Assuming perhaps that I would just go back to the outpost for her lack of credentials. Which is ironic, because back home that would be exactly the sort of thing that people would do, given how in love we were with our qualifications and proper procedures. But I am amongst the barbarians here. I feel I don't need to stand on ceremony. And making Lynesse happy, even inadvertently, is pleasing. Quite beside the anthropological point, say my rational instincts, but at the same time perhaps I will sleep easier tonight with that thrown into the emotional mix.

———————

I awake immediately after my watch system detects that I am being attacked. This is a complex experience made up of (1) a large amount of mostly negative emotional effluvia from my sleep-state transforming into instant adrenaline and panic; (2) a series of top-priority requests from my defensive subsystems requesting me to sign off on various levels of action—up to and including the Terminal Non-Contamination Routines that would be fatal for myself and everyone else within the community.

I actually give the go-ahead to this last, because I have

just awoken and have no idea what is going on. Thankfully, there is no satellite overhead to immediately enact the appropriate devastation, and, in the next second, I send the countermand and catastrophe is averted.

I also manage not to say yes to lethal force, but because three people are pinning me down to the bed and one is in possession of a sharp implement, I OK the rest of the requests and the garments I am sleeping in release a burst of heat, electricity and radiation that send all three shrieking away from me, their skin blistering and their jaws and limbs dancing with galvanic response.

I sit up and stare at them blankly. One of them is the lean proprietor and the other two are large friends of his. On the floor between them is some manner of sawing implement. Even as they run screaming from the room with burned hands and scorched clothes, I reconstruct the moment I awoke into.

They were about to try to saw off my horns. I am truly astonished. I had no idea there was any subculture here that might find a market for such curios. In fact, their loss, were it not that it would require some heavy analgesic support and might interfere with my communications link to the satellites, might even let me blend a little with the locals. Although perhaps that is a fond dream.

By the time I step out of the suddenly vacated hostelry, my assailants have been apprehended. It appears that Lynesse has at last revealed her true nature, and she and Esha have rallied some local constables. When I appear, everyone abruptly defers to me, and I realise that I, as the putative victim of their crimes, am expected to have some hand in the judicial process. This is, of course, just piling contamination on contamination. I am, frankly, not only the last but the worst anthropologist. I'm lucky nobody is coming back to read my reports. I'd be on the first ship home.

The thought of *that* is so bleakly funny that I laugh at it, which silences everyone. I look at the host and his accomplices, who are going to suffer for a long time with their wounds. I honestly don't want to make my failings any worse than they are. I kneel down by them, where they are being held with their faces close to the mud. "I'm afraid you will be in pain for quite a while, and you may suffer long-term neurological damage. And the radiation may well mean you can no longer have children, any of you. In fact, best that nobody goes inside the building for at least seven days to let things subside, OK?" Despite their intentions, it all seems like an overreaction on my part, and I wish I'd kept on clicking through the responses until I reached something more moderate. However, my words make a grand impression on the crowd, in a way I can't understand. Enough that the malefactors are allowed to get up and abscond, apparently punished enough. Which is . . . good? Except I feel that I've just made things worse.

Lynesse seems impressed at my forbearance, though. That lightens my mood a little. I almost feel good-humoured, just in this moment. Perhaps I can leave the DCS to cool off for a little while. I feel . . . *in place,* even if my place is that of the frightening outsider. I am a part of a cultural script that these people understand, and that is a weirdly comforting thought. I have not *belonged* for a long time. As I was the solitary occupant of the outpost, there was nothing to belong to.

Lynesse

THE CROWD WAS PLAINLY not about to disperse any time soon, and so Lyn decided to take control of the situation. She'd already had to reveal just who she was, and she wore the copper gorget at her throat now, marking her out as on royal business. Which she wasn't, of course, but it wouldn't be the first time such trinkets had been misused. It was cold and uncomfortable about her neck, and she would dearly love to be rid of it.

But the people of Wherryover plainly felt they were owed a tale, and Lyn decided that, her cover blown, she may as well capitalise on the situation.

"Yes, I am Fourth Daughter of the Queen, trusted emissary of my mother in times of crisis," because if you were going to lie then make it a big one. "She has heard of the threat arising across the river in the Ordwood, and has called upon her ancient bargains with Nyrgoth Elder, last of the ancient sorcerers. I travel with him now, to confront the demon and banish it back to its twisted realm of darkness!"

Many of her listeners had fled here across the river

from the Ord, and she got a more enthusiastic response than she'd been expecting. The dozen squabbling fiefdoms of the forest were nobody's priority, neither rich nor strategically useful, and usually at one another's throats. The idea that the queen of Lannesite would go further than grudgingly allowing the refugees onto her soil was more than most here had expected. With good reason, as Lyn well knew.

Word would now race back to the palace on burning feet, and her mother would wax marvellous wroth, as the songs had it, but by then Lyn and her companions would be across the water and confronting the demon. And returning home with a confronted demon to her credit would set everything straight, she was sure.

Speeches made, and Esha off securing ferry passage over the river, she approached the sorcerer, who was sitting on a bench outside the inn. He looked up as she approached, and actually smiled, which took her aback. She had grown used to his stern, disapproving expression, as though nothing in the mortal world could truly touch or interest him in any way. Now there was a slight twist at the corner of his mouth, and it made him seem infinitesimally younger and more vulnerable.

They had tried to take his horns. She recalled stories of sorcerous beasts whose horns, when severed, would grant the bearer strange powers or cure maladies, and apparently the villainous innkeeper had believed the same of sorcerers. Her fault, for finding them such wretched digs, but she had hoped to pass through the place without much notice, hiding her own identity in the sorcerer's shadow. When it had all kicked off, she had a moment of utter disgust at her own naivety, at how *bad* she was at this. And then the sorcerer had not even been offended, had taken it all in his solemn stride and not even cared that she was here without royal writ.

"That was a great doom you pronounced on them, Nyrgoth Elder," she said to him respectfully.

His expression—now he *had* expressions—was oddly uncertain. "I don't understand you, Fourth Daughter," he said, in that odd way, titles without proper names so that she wondered if she should just be calling him "Sorcerer" to his face like an insult.

"When you prophesied your attackers would never bear or sire children, and cursed the inn," she prompted. "That was true magic." Probably such things were commonplace to sorcerers, but she had been deeply impressed. To kill someone's entire line with but a word, every generation to come, was a true wizard's retribution. They'd be more careful with their hospitality in Wherry-over from now on.

Nyrgoth Elder looked abruptly irritated. "There is no magic, merely the proper application of universal forces."

Lynesse nodded slowly. That seemed to her to be a scholar's definition of magic, and the sorcerer was suddenly ill-tempered. She had no wish to provoke him even though she didn't quite understand the grounds for his offence.

A moment later he had his blank face back on, that spoke only detachment from her and her ignorance. "I apologise," he told her levelly. "I am not supposed to talk to you of such things." And that, of course, was probably true. Sorcerers were jealous of their secrets.

Esha came back then. "Lyn, all ready to go." She pressed a new sword into Lyn's hands to replace the heirloom the flying monster had ground up. "Ferry wasn't sure whether to charge double for the sorcerer or take us for free." She grinned broadly. "And I have something special I picked up last night. One of the refugees had some piece of the demon. I thought the Elder could take a look at it." She looked enquiringly down at the wizard, who unfolded up from his sitting position. As with all his movements there was neither age nor youth to the movement, as though he was outside time.

On the way to the dock, Esha fell back to match steps with the wizard, and Lyn heard her murmur, "Far be it for me to advise the Elder . . ."

"Speak," from the sorcerer.

"You have not been much amongst people in the long

years since the reign of Astresse Once Regent?"

"That is true."

"To speak a title to one's face, that is ... considered rude. Lynesse Fourth Daughter would not say, but it is as though you consider her a thing. Call me Free Mark when pointing me out to another, yes. Call me Free Mark to my face, you lessen me, as though you cannot spare the time to pick me from my fellows, you see?"

By now Lyn wished her friend had just kept her mouth shut. The sorcerer actually stopped, staring. "Is that the way of it? How was this knowledge kept from me?"

Esha shrugged. "By your separation from the world of men, Nyrgoth Elder. Or so I would guess."

And again, just as after the attack, the Elder was not offended by any of this. In fact, he seemed positively happy to have learned something, and had a little more spring in his stride all the way to the water. Lyn supposed it was rare enough that a sorcerer of the ancient race was taught something new.

The boat crew were three women of Esha's people, bowing to Lyn with that calculated respect the Coast-people used with any notional superior outside their own ranks, that stopped just short of insubordination. They watched the Elder warily, and all held their breath when he stepped aboard the ferry, in case the boat turned to live wood and sprouted leaves, or transformed into a fish.

"Surprised he can't just walk over the water," one of them said, obviously intended to be out of the Elder's hearing, but Nyrgoth turned his head and said brightly, "I suppose I could, but that would be wasteful," and that shut them all up for the voyage.

The thing that Esha had got hold of was nasty looking, more like a claw than anything else. It was a curved spike some six inches long that had obviously been part of some creature, mottled black and green and with the broken end encrusted with what looked like scales. It came wrapped in what had been fine cloth once, and supposedly the seller had been vizier to one of the little forest kingdoms. Easy enough claim to make, Lyn supposed, but it was very fine cloth.

Nyrgoth Elder sat in the belly of the boat with the cloth spread on his lap and studied the thing without touching it, though occasionally he brought his hands close and made what she could only characterise as mystical passes through the air. By the time the far shore approached, he had rewrapped the grisly memento and was frowning a little.

"If I had the assistance of my tower I could probably make more of this," he told her. "I think your friend may have been lied to, though. I can see no artificial structures within it at all. It's not a relic of the ancient times, as Ulmoth possessed. Your people may have been scared off by some animal new to their forest."

Lyn held on to that as they disembarked, and held on to it as Esha paid the boat crew and the vessel put off. She even managed to hold on to it as they wove through the tent-cluttered space that had been the market grounds on the Ordwood river side, turning her face from the plight of the hundreds who had come this far and no farther. The anger was building up inside her all that time, though, and she felt her control over it fraying from moment to moment. She wanted to make a scene right there, where all those displaced people could hear her. She wanted them to share just what she thought of the sorcerer's words, and join her in her condemnation.

Nyrgoth Elder was patently unaware of her reaction, and so when she finally couldn't hold it in any longer—after they were clear of the camp and into the trees—she caught him entirely off guard when she rounded on him.

"No, I do *not* think that all those people were driven out of their homes by an animal!" she snapped at him. "Nor do I believe, Nyrgoth Elder, that the forest folk, who for all their lives, and the lives of their ancestors, have known these lands, would have a single beast within these trees that they did not recognise, be it predator or prey. I believe there is a demon, as they say, and that it controls minds and feeds on people and cannot be fought by normal ways. Otherwise I would not have risked my mother's wrath and my own life by trekking to your tower and calling on our family's compact. It is sorcery that needs sorcery to fight it! Not an animal that needs only a bow and a spear!"

She ended up shouting quite loudly, and broke off, horrified at how impolitic she had abruptly become. Inside, she knew with utter misery that what she was *really* railing against was her mother and her court, because they had said exactly the same thing as the sorcerer. And if, just *if*, they and Nyrgoth were correct, and there was no demon nor sorcery, then she had done an incalculably foolish thing and confirmed everybody's bad opinion of her forever.

For a moment there was an expression on his face—such an expression: panic, horror, hurt, offence and fear all crammed into those aquiline features, and none of them looks that a sorcerer's visage should bear. Then all trace of it was gone, as completely as if she had been entirely mistaken, and his haughty, unruffled stare was back. She waited for him to just go, perhaps walking across the water as he'd said, or disappearing into thin air.

"I'm sorry," she whispered, for a moment just her child-self standing before any number of broken vases and windows, knowing the sentiments were too little and too late. The words bounced off his stiff regard, but then he inclined his head slightly, a superior accepting the contrition of an inferior, which she supposed was her due.

"The apologies are mine, Lyn," he told her. "These are your rituals. It's not for me to detract from them. We should continue to hunt this demon of yours."

Lynesse froze, feeling horribly awkward again. Nothing the sorcerer said or did ever seemed to be quite right, and did he think she didn't understand that he was humouring her? "Yes," she got out, forcing a smile to her face. "We shall. And we'll avoid towns, where we can."

Nyr

ESHA FREE MARK IS a fascinating case. Her Fisher-people arose from first-generation biomodification amongst the colonists. The original records I have seen make no mention of any plan for it to be inheritable, but someone obviously decided that being able to breathe and see underwater was worth its energy cost. Esha's lungs can switch to a high-efficiency mode suitable to extract the low levels of oxygen dissolved in water. She is also considerably paler than most of the natives of this part of the world and I imagine she pays for it in sunburn and skin problems. In respect of my own field, the Fisher-people are an autonomous ethnic group that crosses state boundaries at will using the waterways, and gives no explicit fealty to any government. This lets them fulfil a useful role as traders, messengers and emissaries, as well, I suspect, as spying and smuggling. Their protection from persecution lies with the proportion of the trade routes that rely on their watercraft. Any state that took action against them en masse would find itself starved of goods and funds.

This background, with its freedom of travel and its exposure to countless acts of petty diplomacy, has led to someone like Esha. She has by her own report lived a life of travel, mostly away from her people and their rivers. She's plainly a linguist and has been trying to tease some of my native speech from me, hunting out the similarities with their own web of languages here. Which similarities are limited to the most basal, human words, but they are there and she's sharp enough to spot them. She is highly intelligent, and knows the land we travel well, albeit from before this "demon" came. Lyn has engaged her services not just as guide but as companion. I'd say "chaperone," but I recall from my dealings with Astresse that women of the ruling, fighting and itinerant classes are generally better trained in the martial skills than their menfolk. Farm and artisan women take fewer risks, I recall, but the upper classes traditionally spend the blood of their womenfolk profligately, and often adopt heirs into their lineages to replace the losses. Leading to a socially mobile society where the rise of a meritorious commoner like Esha raises no eyebrows.

We are three days out from the river, and things are awkward between us, which is why I have been spending time updating my professional notes. Lyn perhaps still feels badly about her outburst, just as I would be stinging for my own insensitivity if I'd let the DCS off its leash for even a moment since it happened. I have tried to make peace with her, but every time I speak her name or address her she throws up her own shields, putting on an expression that I took initially for cheer but now realise is entirely forced. Apparently, I am still doing this all wrong. I have tried to think what was different with Astresse, but the answer is "everything," so no help there. Remembering that Lyn is not Astresse is easy enough under Dissociative Cognition, but the resemblance is so striking that I fear for my sanity if I have to bring the shield down. And I will have to bring it down soon and wallow in my own emotions, which my readouts suggest are very negative indeed and haven't lightened up since leaving the river.

And I do not, truly, know why we are here. Is there actually a beast? Is there some warlord, even though the thing Esha had shown me had nothing of old colonial technology to it? Or is this some ritual venture that I have been brought along for, perhaps the youngest child proving herself by acting out some legend? Perhaps the demon is in her mind only. To say so is patently taboo, though.

We have been travelling through dense forest, along trails only Esha can see, and I suspect the lack of direct sun is adding to the general sense of oppression I am staving off, not to mention interfering with the recharging of my clothes and internal systems. I need to find a chance to get away from the others, even for just a night, so I can let the DCS up. My body has been working under the sour biochemistry of all those gut feelings, meaning that a considerable debt has arisen, a gap between mind and matter, so to speak. The longer I leave it before finding my own equilibrium, the worse the come-down will be. I can't just keep staving it off. I find myself experiencing moments of panic and anxiety that have no immediate cause, because the prompt that generated them came and went hours or even days before. They arise and paralyse my mind for whole minutes, all the harder to deal with because they are shorn of context. I feel as though the emotional parts of my mind are like a cellar in which I have locked dead things, and when I open the door . . . maggots, carrion flies, flooding out. And yet I must, because the latch and hinges are strained already.

"Lyn," I say at last. "I must . . ." I am going to lie to her. "I must go and study the stars." A risible fabrication, but she nods, that strained smile on her face again.

"Of course, Nyrgoth Elder." Her eyes creep sideways to find Esha. "Ahead there is Watacha, the city-state. Last we heard Elhevesse Regent still held power there, and may grant us aid or even troops. Study the stars tonight, seek your portents, and we will make Watacha by noon tomorrow. Does that suit your purposes, Nyrgoth?"

"Nyr," I tell her. "My name is Nyr. Nyr Illim Tevitch." Not even an abbreviation, but I don't see why I should be saddled with a suffix like some winter coat if everyone else is doffing them.

That taut expression twitches and pulls tighter across her face. Apparently, that was the wrong thing to say, again. I am fighting off more emotional bleed, though, frustration and anger and sorrow, none of which are actually germane to what we're talking about. Except that, perhaps, I just want to go by my real name, just once.

——————

That evening I discover Esha really does know the land because, without ever having made any obvious diversion, we find a clearing in the forest, the first we've observed. This is man-made, some manner of timber felling or charcoal burning or some other pastoral pursuit. I said I wanted to observe the stars, and they took me at my word. I feel another block of guilt slot unacknowledged into the grand tower of hurt about to fall on me, that I've made them work on false pretences.

"I will need to be alone here, for scholarly reasons," I explain to them. "Return to me after dawn."

They exchange glances, and I cannot parse what passes

between them. Lyn says, "What if the beast catches up with you?"

I am adrift. "Your demon?"

"Your beast, that follows you." She is frowning, and the words come out a little like a recital. "That you spoke of."

For quite a long time I have absolutely no idea what she is talking about, mind blank, and she and I just stare at each other. Then my linguistic helper systems kick in and I realise what she means.

"That is why I must be alone tonight," I explain to them. "I need to confront matters before they grow too strong." I am trying to recall my precise wording, speaking to her before, and now I am not sure if she thinks there is a literal beast or not, just as I am not sure if her "demon" is real or just symbolic. I want to sit her down and explain things to her, but the effort involved seems insuperable and I am becoming aware that my understanding of both language and culture here is simply inadequate, despite centuries of information gathering.

They leave me in the clearing, though, and at least I know that my defences are more than equal to any actual beast that might come along. So sayeth the disassociated intellectual brain with its vaunted objectivity.

I sit in the clearing's heart, on the trunk of a fallen tree deemed, I assume, unsuitable for timber, and disable the DCS.

Ah, well, not so bad then. I can sit here and be quite philosophical about the whole business. I mean, it's an adventure, isn't it? More, despite the risk of cultural contamination, Rule One in the good anthropological practice manual we all had to sign, I'm learning more about my subjects of study than any amount of clandestine drone recordings and eavesdropping. When I get back to the outpost, I'll have the mother of all reports to file. I can spend happy hours going over all my previous work and rubbishing it for my academic community of one, because what else is there, precisely? When this is done, what's waiting for me but the echoes within that tower and the staticky silence of the comms, and the cold suspension bed, and the centuries?

Sutler and Bennaw and Porshai went home when they were called, but we all told one another it was a temporary matter. I can remember how excited we all were at how the work was going here. Better to leave someone to gather data so that we could all throw ourselves into the study when they came back. I was more than happy to volunteer. I had suspension and the satellite and it wasn't going to be for *long*. A few wakings and sleepings for me, a few generations for the locals. But locals die, and that's just a part of the study. We can see how they treat their dead and write bright little dissertations on what we think it means, and never actually know what it means or how it feels for them. Because that's not what anthropology is for. It's not for knowing how it is to live as a native of Sophos 4, or any of these diasporic human colonies flung out into the cold abyss of space by a desperately optimistic humanity. No, it's for writing coolly academic papers, DCS engaged for maximum objectivity, about the possible meanings of the red stylised faces they put on cremation urns. I have written up seventeen different cultural pathways for this image to have taken, most of which take as a starting point the logo of one of the colonial contractors from way back when, which bears a distinct resemblance to the funerary marker. How did a manufacturer of clothing become a harbinger of death? Hmm, yes, all so academically interesting. And of course the one thing I wasn't to do was go and *ask* because what could the locals possibly know about it? And I wrote great reams of nonsense, and now I can look back on it, with a very different kind of objectivity, and say, as my formal conclusion to the body of my academic work, that it's all utter fucking nonsense. Most likely it would have been of no interest or relevance to anyone even had the others ever returned, even had the comms not just dwindled to goddamn silence and never spoken again. But now, *now,* what good is anything I've done and what good is anything I am, when nobody's coming back for me, and when nothing I have is of any relevance to any other human being on this planet?

They think I'm a wizard. They think I'm a fucking wizard. That's what I am to them, some weird goblin man from another time with magic powers. And I literally do not have the language to tell them otherwise. I say, "scientist," "scholar," but when I speak to them, in their language, these are both cognates for "wizard." I imagine myself standing there speaking to Lyn and saying, "I'm not a wizard; I'm a wizard, or at best a wizard." It's not funny. I have lived a long, long life and it has meant nothing, and now I'm on a fucking *quest* with a couple of women who don't understand things like germs or fusion power or anthropological theories of value.

And I am absolutely intellectually able to agree, yes, all of this great crashing wave of negative feeling is not actually being caused by the things I am pinning it to. This is something generated by my biochemistry, grown in my basal brain and my liver and my gut and let loose to roam like a faceless beast about my body until it reaches my cognitive centres, which look around for the worry du jour and pin that mask on it. I know that, while I have real problems in the world, they are not causing the way I feel within myself, this crushing weight, these sudden attacks of clenching fear, the shakes, the wrenching vertiginous horror that doubles me over. These feelings are just recruiting allies of convenience from my rational mind, like a mob lifting up a momentary demagogue who may be discarded a moment later in favour of a better. Even in the grip of my feelings I can still acknowledge all this, and it doesn't help. *Know thyself,* the wise man wrote, and yet I know myself, none better, and the knowledge gives me no power.

I've done the grand tour of the interplanetary situation, always a favourite when I'm casting about for reasons for why I feel so bad. It leaves me hollow, without energy. I've gone off the log now, lying on my side on the ground curled up into a ball. I've never cared about religion, aside from as a subject of study in others, but in my blackest pits of despair I always find God and call out for help, because only an omnipotent outside force could possibly move the stone that is pressing me down. And God walks away, single footsteps off into the collective unconscious. He doesn't care. Why should he? I wouldn't.

For a moment I can almost come to terms with it all, a brief respite, and probably I should have turned the DCS back on then, except the problem is I don't want to. You'd think it'd be a no-brainer, really. You'd think I'd never turn the fucking thing *off*. It's built with safeguards that bug you when you haven't let off steam in a while, though, so eventually you have to do what I'm doing now, and I've already left it too long. What's counterintuitive is, because I'm such a fuck-up, when I'm in the pits, some part of me doesn't want to climb out. Yes, it's bloody awful down here, but at the same time nobody's making demands of me, not even myself. If I put the DCS back on and get up and go back to Lyn and Esha then I'll have to *do* something. I'll have to do my bloody awful pointless job, and I'll have to go on this stupid, meaningless journey with them, and every moment will be awkward and strained and wrong.

Because Astresse is dead and it's not the same. There, a new brick to add to the tower of recrimination. Astresse Regent, who was fierce and bold and beautiful, who took a brief month of my life and lit it up, is dead, long dead, died while I slept, and then her descendants died, too, and then theirs grew old. And intellectually I know that I was still dealing with these problems when I was with her, but in the treacherous light of hindsight she was glorious like the sun, but a sun whom my memory honours only by noting how bloody dark it's got now she's gone.

And yes, all the minor chorus starts up, about how Astresse was also the source of my worst unprofessionalism, and how I'd be hauled up for it should anyone come back and check up on me, and how nobody's coming back to check up on me, and how . . . but it's not even these humdrum woes that grip me the worst. It's that she's dead, and I will never have those days back, when I did stupid, stupid things, unbecoming of a serious academic, and rode to war at the side of a warrior queen whom, despite absurd differences in age and culture and genetic makeup, I loved.

That breaks me, or perhaps it breaks my depression, or both of us. Abruptly the sobs are coming, and then I'm just lying there in a forest clearing in a world where they've forgotten everything they ever knew about space travel, bawling my eyes out like a child because of a woman I knew for a fragment of time so brief, in relation to all the life I've lived, that she may as well never have existed.

It is cathartic; it is exhausting. And I sleep at last, my demons run as ragged as their prey.

In the morning there is a blanket over me. I could probably find a positive interpretation of this, if I could fight my way clear of the clouds, but instead I know it just means that Lyn and Esha were watching. Probably they had blades in hand because they thought there was a real beast they could fight off. Instead of a fight, they got to see their vaunted wizard weeping and trembling like a child, and that is just one more thing to feel physically sick about.

I lie there for a long time in the wan sunlight, on the wet ground, fighting over whether to engage the DCS. To make that decision is to get over a hill that seems insurmountable. Easier by far to let the negative feelings have the run of the place, to stay huddled in the last latched cupboard of my mind.

But at last, somehow, I give the command, which was designed to be as easy as possible for just this reason. And, yes, ready to meet the day now, thank you. Get up, feel my clothes already drying themselves out. We are to go to another community now, and this time as formal demon-hunters to meet with the local government. And I shall stay at the back and make notes and everything can go into the reports. Good. Yes.

My readouts suggest that last night's excesses didn't make much of a dent in my emotional balance, which is always the problem with such things. It's not as though the whole business of depression is a zero-sum game, after all. But for now I can function again, and bleed-over should be minimal. I will just keep myself calm and avoid unnecessary provocation.

I return to Lyn and Esha at their camp. They are looking at me, and I scan their faces for things like pity or disgust, just to get that out of the way. Instead, they seem oddly impressed, and I realise that I've found another hole in my understanding. Theirs is not an overtly emotional culture. There are strict rules about intimacy and formality. What does it mean, for a grown person to have a full-on emotional meltdown? What does it mean when that adult is of a peculiar status such as mine? I have absolutely no idea, but apparently it is ... creditable, in some way. Perhaps it is a luxury accorded only to certain social roles, either the powerful or extreme outsiders. Perhaps I have some secondary function as a lightning rod for tantrums, so that other people can maintain face.

Watacha has wooden walls, and was probably built to house perhaps a thousand people, up on a hill long cleared of trees and with the best view possible of the surrounding land, given that everything is cloaked in trees. The various little forest feudalities have small populations and no field agriculture at all, instead cultivating the forest itself so that hard lines between nature and the work of human hands are often hard to discern. The hill is thronging with tents and makeshift shelters, evidence of some serious population displacement, demonic or otherwise. I do still wonder if they might be giving personhood to some natural force, a pestilence or crop disease, or even a political schism. The way their languages work, with their multitude of qualifiers, means that I have difficulty telling metaphors from literal reports. Nothing is ever simply itself, in their speech.

Lyn's rank signifiers get us admitted. Inside the walls,

the city is crowded and the armed women who met us at the gate have to shove and elbow their way through the streets. I have to mute my olfactory senses after a while, because the stench of too many people and not enough water becomes intolerable. This place will be rife with disease soon, if it isn't already.

We are met not by Elhevesse Regent but by a woman of close to Lyn's age, sitting on a carved wooden throne too large for her. She is Jerevesse Third Daughter. The language she speaks is related to Lyn's, strangely accented and peppered with loan words from several other language groups, so that I have to work hard to translate what she says. My internal lexicons do their best to fill in gaps, but the dialect is unfamiliar, and so I am always an exchange behind as the women address each other.

I am watching Lyn, and she takes being met by this Third Daughter hard. At first I think we all thought that Elhevesse just doesn't take any of us seriously, but no. Elhevesse took a number of soldiers west into the forest five days ago, to confront the demon. Since then, no word has come from them.

Lyn just stands there, digesting the news. She stands very straight and her face is very calm, and Jerevesse sits regally enough, and her face, too, is very calm, and Esha stands somewhat back and looks down so that her face, calm or not, is in shadow. And I suddenly see, as though a book had opened, all the little tells that show just how emotional they are being. The child-queen Third Daughter's steepled fingers are white with the pressure they exert on one another. Lyn's fists are clenched into knotted balls with a tension entirely absent from her face. We are just a few days too late and everything has been lost. This, then, was the plan, but nobody consulted the queen of Watacha about it, and now there is no army, just a great number of hungry, sick, frightened people.

"Who have you brought, though?" Jerevesse says. "Who stands like a shadow at your back?"

I think she means Esha at first, but of course she means me.

Lyn rallies at this. She has no army, but she has a magician. She names me for the Third Daughter, and I am somewhat alarmed at the weight our host gives to this pronouncement.

"He can defeat the demon?"

"In my great-grandmother's time his powers cast down Ulmoth and destroyed his monstrous followers. He is the last of the ancient race of makers," Lyn says, glancing at me with such hope and wonder that I almost look over my shoulder to see what superman she has seen there. My readouts spike: probably I should be flattered, but my natural, suppressed reaction to all this is to feel sick about it. I put up a hand to forestall any more, but it is too late.

"This is a great matter," Jerevesse says. "My people have been days knowing only defeat."

"Then let us bring victory," Lyn says immediately. She has lit up, because she is being taken seriously, but the only reason is me, and I am not . . . I am not . . .

I am impassive. I am clinical. What a fascinating folk ritual, yes. Worthy of a footnote when I return to the outpost. "Primitive Beliefs and the Negative Results Thereof," a monograph by Nyr Illim Tevitch, anthropologist second class.

Lynesse

LOOKING ON THE SORCERER'S impassive features, Lyn envied him his calm. She would trade a night of agony and weeping for being able to face up to failure while the sun shone. And yes, she had crept back to spy on him, with her new sword in hand in case there was a beast. She had seen his mask come off. There was a story she had been told as a child, about a magician who lived for a hundred years, and every dawn he was handsome and unlined as a youth of four Storm-seasons, but (as his unwary bride discovered) each night he aged all of his years, all at once, becoming a wizened, stick-limbed horrible thing. Nyrgoth Elder did not age, for all that he had seen out his centuries. Instead, what came on him at night was what she could only assume to be a lifetime's dread and fear and anguish, all the little emotions that little people had to battle, but which a sorcerer, it seemed, could just put aside for later. She felt horribly guilty for violating his trust, bitterly envious of this new demonstration of his power. It was not a magic spoken of in stories, and yet right then it seemed more useful than any casting of the lightning or commanding of monsters.

Esha had also spied on the sorcerer, Lyn had discovered shortly before he rejoined them. Worse, she had laid a blanket over Nyrgoth Elder, because the Coast-people would never dream of letting a travelling companion go without. Which meant the man knew they had not kept to their word, which made it hard to face him, even though he hadn't seemed to care.

And then he was still calling her by her familiar name, shorn of her honorific, and now even asking her to call him likewise, and that was worse, so that she was thinking of that storybook sorcerer who, despite his power had still wanted a princess for his table companion and his bed. She was waiting for the moment when she called upon his power and he named his price. She had, after all, put herself into just such a story by knocking at the door of his tower. She should have remembered how such tales went. *And I am caught in it now, and cannot just change my mind. The wizard is right here.*

And so she would have to make the most capital she could of it, before he turned that sternly dispassionate visage to her and made his demands. She could, at least, bring a little light back to the people of Watacha.

She wondered who the real Jerevesse Third Daughter was, behind the mask of civic responsibility. Was she another delinquent heir, not close enough to inheriting to be valuable, not trusted enough to go with her mother? Or was she the devoted and dutiful daughter, always being passed over for important tasks and yet a diligent keeper of the keys while others made state visits or met with diplomats? No way to find out, not with things as they were.

This next part was going to be the easy bit, though. Jerevesse had sent out heralds to proclaim a Petitioners' Circle—outside the walls, because there was nowhere within the city that so many could assemble. By the time Lyn and her companions arrived, a scaffold had been raised for them to stand on, and a grand crowd had gathered, likely more than Lyn's mother had ever needed to address at once. *Yes, for a mere headcount, very impressive, but Mother never had such a desperate audience either.* Usually the Circle was because some group or other had a grievance, against the court, against other citizens, against brigands or foreigners. Representatives chosen beforehand would step forwards and recite how the problem had affected them, with the clear implication that the Crown should be doing something about it. After they were done, the queen or her representative would make a considered response, accepting, rejecting, proposing. Sometimes the Circle would be back the next day, the petitioners explaining how the suggested action would be insufficient to remedy their woes; sometimes the queen's speaker would make it plain that some woes were to be endured. As the woes were frequently tax related, this was not uncommon, but overall such Circles were a part of any state's good governance, and the ruler who ignored them or refused to call them was risking less lawful means of expression.

Jerevesse at least did her own speaking. She stood on the scaffold and called to her people, and heralds at intervals within the crowd passed on her words. She expressed a profound hope that her mother and the soldiers would return with good news shortly, which wish everyone plainly shared and nobody believed in. Then she gestured at Lyn and announced, "The plight of the Ord has not been ignored by those beyond our borders. Not every back has been turned against us. I bring before you Lynesse Fourth Daughter of Lannesite, most powerful and resplendent of our eastern neighbours!" Larding the bread a bit thick there, because Lannesite seldom got on well with the forest kingdoms and usually tried to play them off against one another. The crowd was less than impressed, but Jerevesse was not done.

"'Where are the soldiers of Lannesite?' you have asked," she declared, and Lyn shuffled uneasily, because that was plainly what a lot of them were indeed asking. "Where is the gleaming armour and the Firebird banner?" Jerevesse went on, and held her hands up to forestall the growing murmur of discontent. "I ask you, if the ranks of Lannesite had come across the river to us, how glad would you truly have been, to see them? How long before you would have asked your neighbour, 'When will they leave, do you think?' And every court and nation has its ill-thinkers. I know that if our own army was within the walls of Lannesite Urban then some would ask, 'Why must *we* leave?'"

She even managed to spur a little murmur of humour with that barb, and Lyn decided that the Third Daughter had been left behind because of her skills and not her deficiencies. *Not like me at all, then.*

"Instead, Lannesite brings to our aid something of more worth than swords or arrows," Jerevesse continued. "More even than the silver blood of their royal house who stands before you. Stand forth, petitioners; bring Lynesse Fourth Daughter your complaints."

For a moment Lyn expected everyone to just rush forwards, all shouting at once, but Jerevesse's people had done their work well, and three people shuffled forwards from the throng, fewer than might be expected even for a dispute over the taxation of melons. The first was an old man, stooped but still broad across the shoulders, his face leathered by a life out of doors.

"The demon came to my orchards and turned my livelihood against me," he declared, looking from Lyn to the people around him. "Many here'll tell the same story. When the fruit began to show on the bough, it was unnatural, wrong shape, wrong colours. Before harvest time, we could see it moving. Thought it was some pest got inside it. We burned the worst, but it was everywhere." He was calm, saying all this: words spoken a dozen times already, become rote. "Then it was moving, like it was gone from plant to beast, crawling down the trunks. Then the trees that had borne such fruit, they withered and died where the things had fed off them. And then all the things the demon devoured came to feed off us, and we had nothing left, and we fled." He nodded once, his job done, and stepped back a pace.

The next petitioner was a broad woman, looking haggard from lack of sleep. She had to croak a few times before she could get the words out strongly enough to be heard, and even then one of the court stood at the foot of the scaffold to relay everything.

"The demon came to our village," Lyn heard. "At first it was the cerkitts and the other beasts. The demon got into them, from what they ate, or from the bites they got when they went into the trees. Things grew on them, like eyes, like crystals. They went feral, and whoever was bitten by them, or just was too long near them, they got it, too. My own sons went to cull the herds of the rot, but some never came back, and some came back but weren't themselves. The demon had taken them for its own."

There was more to be said there, but her nerve broke and she, too, stepped back, which left a thin, scarred man standing out from the crowd. His left hand was wrapped in rags, and when he moved to free it, Lyn thought she would see the mark of the demon the woman had spoken of. Instead, though, he raised a hand short all its fingers and marked with the broken tree brand, meaning he was a criminal cast out from his home.

"Some of you know me." His voice was surprisingly strong. "I am Allwerith Exiled, and in any other season it'd be death for me to stand here." Indeed, there were plenty of bleak looks at him from his neighbours. "The Third Daughter's people chose me to speak here because no others here saw what I saw. Because I had fled to Farbourand to get from under the shadow of my judgment here at Watacha."

Lyn consulted her inner map and reckoned Farbourand was a frontier sort of place, one of the lawless outposts where trappers and prospectors came to resupply before heading out into the wilds again.

"I saw where the demon came first," Allwerith declared. "A certain clearing near that place, where all the trees were overrun with its spawn, where all the beasts, great and small, had been slaved to it, and made into its bricks and timbers, for the things it was building there. I saw circles and great cords growing from the earth, and all of it set over with spines and black eyes. And men, too, all part of it, doing its will or being pieces of its creation. And none at Farbourand believed me, and then the demon came, with men and beasts all made to do its will, and none got out but I. And I came to Birchari and warned them, and they beat me out with switches for the lies they said I told. And there are some here who escaped Birchari who will give the truth of my words. And I came here, and I praise Elhevesse Regent and I praise Jenevesse Third Daughter and all their servants, for here I was believed."

He clenched his one fist, the stumps of the other hand twitching, and stepped back into the silence. Jenevesse cocked an eye at Lyn, who swallowed.

She tried to remember how her mother did it: address such a great assembly, sound poised and certain, not the frightened child so far out of her depth. Her heart was hammering, but she heard the voices of her tutors in her head and took hold of her breathing, levelling and slowing it, picking people from the crowd to look in the eye, nodding, spreading her hands to show her sincerity.

"News of the Ordwood's plight has reached Lannesite, as you hear," she told them, and heard her own voice steady and clear. At the corner of her vision, Esha gave her a nod of approval.

"It is an ill time for all when evil magic is loose in the world," she told them, "and threats such as this demon cannot go unanswered. But we have seen such magic before, in the hands of monsters and evil men. We all of us have heard a tale of Lucef Half-Elder, in whose day the land was plagued with monstrous beasts, some that destroyed and others that simply poisoned the world with their presence. And Lucef, who was wise in the ways of sorcery, destroyed each one or bound it with strong words so that it would not trouble his people. Lucef, it is said, was born half of our people and half of the ancient strain of makers, so that even as a child his understanding of the secrets of the world was beyond the ken of wise men." And yes, everyone knew the Lucef stories, or their own version of them. So: "Let me tell you, then, of my own ancestor, Astresse Once Regent, when her land was threatened by the sorcerer warlord Ulmoth, who had raised from deathly sleep some of those beasts that Lucef bound. Ulmoth brought his army of monsters and madmen onto the soil of Lannesite, but the Once Regent knew that craft must be fought with craft.

"In that time of need she braved the journey to the Tower of the Elders, where dwelled the last of that line, Nyrgoth, and he rode alongside her and used his words of power to bind Ulmoth's beasts and send them back to the earth." More and more eyes were flicking to the sorcerer's tall, silent presence at her shoulder. She saw the current of understanding ripple out through the crowd, mouth to ear, people craning their heads for a better view of the man's twisted horns and not-quite-human features. She saw hope break like the dawn sun over hills.

"I have brought no armies," she confirmed to them. "I have brought the great sorcerer himself to confront the demon and break its hold over these lands. With his craft and his power he will go to its lair and break its grip over your sons and daughters; he will purge its taint from your orchards and pacify the corrupted beasts of the forest. He is Nyrgoth Elder, last of the ancients, of a race whose very thoughts are magic such as no human wizard ever dreamt of." And she was seeing wide eyes, smiles, the desperate need to believe in her, in *her*, Lynesse Fourth Daughter, least valued of her line. For just a moment she could forget all that had gone before, all the years of falling short of the standards demanded by her mother and demonstrated by her siblings.

I am doing this, she realised. *I have found my place.* She would go back to her mother in triumph. She would be given honours and responsibilities fit for a princess. She would be the champion of her line, the wonder of the age.

"We will drive the demon back to the otherworld it came from!" she declared to them. "We will free your homes from its corruption! For Watacha and Ordwood, for Lannesite and the world!"

They cheered her. They actually cheered her, enough that Jerevesse Third Daughter gave her a worried look, as though fearing that there might be a change of ruling house in the city sometime soon. And while Lyn had no plans in that direction, it was refreshing to be taken seriously.

Nyrgoth himself said nothing, and his hooded eyes showed nothing of what he might think or feel. He simply shadowed her heels back to the palace at Watacha, to the suite of rooms Jenevesse had prepared for them. It was agreed that they would set out for the lands of the demon the next day, and Lyn had asked if the criminal Allwerith could be found for them, because despite his pedigree his knowledge seemed useful.

Only when they were behind closed doors did Esha say, "You might have overdone it."

"It was what they wanted to hear," Lyn told her carelessly.

"'Want and need are distant cousins,'" Esha quoted.

"What," broke in Nyrgoth Elder's stern voice, "was that?"

She started. Caught up by her own words, she had almost forgotten that he was a thinking, living thing, rather than some legendary weapon she would wield. His face was . . . immobile, more so even than usual, as though it had become a mask carved from sallow wood.

She made an enquiring sound, abruptly wrong-footed, unable to see where he was coming from.

"Do you understand what you have promised these people?" the sorcerer asked her.

Still not understanding him, she set her shoulders. Perhaps this was a test, in the way of wizards. "You have promised me your aid, according to your compact with my blood. I told you of the demon, and you came with me here to defeat it. And we will. Your magic will overcome it, Nyrgoth Elder, and then all will be well and everyone will be saved." She had been about to force out his personal name, to call him "Nyr" as though they were companions of old or something more, but her nerve failed her on that score.

The sorcerer stared at her for an uncomfortable span of time, and she braced herself. *I had forgotten the price, of course. Here it comes.* But what he said next was so far from what she expected that she actually staggered, as though trying to force an open door. No demands of flesh or fealty, but only:

"There is no magic."

She and Esha goggled at him, and eventually Esha said, "Nygoth Elder, we have seen you curse a man to barrenness and dominate a flying monster with mere words."

The sorcerer looked from one to the other. "This, what you have told them, it is not fair, nor true. There is no universal magic that can accomplish these things. When it was just your stories and your journeys, I held my peace. That is what I'm supposed to do, after all. I am supposed to let you people get on with your traditions and your beliefs and just note it all down. But these people are desperate." His voice was dreadfully flat, the lack of emotion in it positively crying out. She had the sense of something huge and buried rising towards the surface like a sea monster about to break a fishing boat across its back. "They are hungry and sick, hurt, displaced. And you have given them false hope on the back of a story about magic. There is no magic."

"I . . ." She tried a smile. "Nyrgoth Elder, you are testing me. I have faith in you. You will be able to defeat the demon."

She saw the precise moment when something broke inside him, and all that mastery of himself was just cast aside. "No!" he snapped, and most of what he was radiating was sheer frustration. "There is no such thing as magic, you stupid girl. There are no such things as demons. There is only the way the world works. I come from a people who understand the world, and so there are things we can accomplish with it that you cannot. I know of the ancient words to command the servants and workers of elder days, like that wise fool Ulmoth un-earthed. I have items of power which can chastise my enemies and protect me. There is no magic. I am not a magician, but a wizard." He grimaced. "Not a wizard but a sorcerer, a magus. A . . ." And he said a word she had never heard, sharp and alien sounding, unsettling as metal on a tooth. And then a tirade, a whole sentence of the same words cast upwards, past the ceiling to the un-caring sky. A wizard's curse.

She and Esha waited for transformations, plagues, horrors. But apparently, whatever the curse was, it would come to light on them later, not now. Now was for Nyr-goth Elder to stare at her, his hands crooked into terrible claws, his square, white teeth bared, eyes bulging.

"There is no such thing as magic. I don't care about the rules. I don't care what I'm supposed to say and not say. I can't let you just use my name to lie to all those people out there. I don't know what this demon of theirs is, save that there are no demons. For all I know, it's some nat-ural process of this world, something that arises once in a thousand years, and something I have no way of influ-encing. Something that just happens, only now it's hap-pening and there are humans here in the way. And if it's that, then I can't help. I don't think I can help anyway. I'm not a wizard; I'm . . ." He deflated, for a moment the most forlorn thing she'd ever seen, not the Elder sorcerer but some misshapen prodigy from a travelling show. Then the rage was back without warning, and he slammed his fists into the wall hard enough that he left bloody smears where the skin over his knuckles had broken. Lyn flinched and heard her own whimper in the silence that followed, but Esha just pointed at Nyrgoth's hands, where the skin was visibly knitting, torn edges crawling together and leaving no sign nor scar.

"It's not magic," he insisted, against all reason. "I am just made this way. I am just of a people who understand how the world works."

"Nyrgoth Elder," Esha said slowly. "Is that not what magic is? Every wise man, every scholar I have met who pretended to the title of magician, that was their study. They sought to learn how the world worked, so that they could control and master it. That is magic."

"No!" he insisted. "A spade is not magic, just because it turns the earth better than your fingers! Iron is not magic, just because it needs a smith's skill to forge. It is just knowledge." Abruptly he was pressing his hands to his face. "No, no, I've already ... I shouldn't be here. I shouldn't have interfered. It was different with Ulmoth. This isn't any of my business. I'm ... doing it wrong."

"Nyrgoth Elder, great sorcerer, please," Lyn said hurriedly. "In the name of your vow to Astresse Once Regent, you are needed here. That is your duty."

"My duty is to let you all die," he told her, not even harshly but with a terrible misery, the sadness of hundreds of years. "I should just walk away and let this happen, and record the story of it for those to come, as though there is anyone who will ever come. I should not be here. I am not a part of your stories."

"But Ulmoth—"

"Ulmoth was different," he told her, but then: "Ulmoth wasn't different, though. I told myself it was my business, that he was interrupting the natural way of things here, because he had raised the ancient workers to cause trouble. But your whole world is built on the backs of those workers. How was what he did any more or less natural than your people running about with swords and kingdoms? The whole *point* of us coming here was a lie. There is no natural state. You're a colony." He was sunk in a different despair now, that same beast that he had fought in the forest, the one within him.

Lyn exchanged a look with Esha. "I don't understand you," she said softly, and then, "Nyr," because when he was weak and unhappy that seemed an easier thing to say.

"I'm going to tell you, then." He looked up and the smile he gave her was horrible, fragile. "Sit and listen, children, for I will tell you the true story of your people and your world, and break every law of my people. I don't care anymore. Just listen."

Nyr and Lynesse

About fifteen hundred years ago your ancestors came to this planet from another, a place called Earth. They came in a spaceship and the journey lasted many generations. On that ship they slept and woke, had children, died, until the last generation was trained by the ship in how to start the colonisation process. They were part of a wave of colonisation from Earth, the great dream of expanding into the universe.

Nearly four hundred Storm-seasons past, the ancients brought men into this world from the otherworld, ferrying them upon a boat through the seas of night in a voyage so long that those who left one shore were dust and their children's children had to be taught how to farm and hunt and govern by the ship's figurehead, which spoke with many voices and told them of a hundred ships and a hundred shores. In this way they became the living dream of the ancients.

They landed and set about adapting this planet for their purposes. It was already similar to the planet they had left,

When their ship beached they came ashore to a land that did not know them, but they were the ancients and with their

and there was a functioning ecosystem here, things like plants and animals, though without the hard dividing lines that they had known on Earth. The engineers of those people changed themselves and their environment, melding Earth and native stock to insert themselves into the planetary ecosystem, so that what you have now, your crops, your beasts, some are natives and some are tweaked Earth creatures and others are hybrids of the two, so that there is precious little left that resembles the original alien ecosystem.

All of this was done in the understanding that the vastly expensive endeavour of interstellar colonisation would be self-sustaining and go on forever, as people so often think that the structures and systems they build will go on for-

magic they set about teaching the beasts and plants their place, naming them and giving them their roles. Those beasts and plants that would serve, they rewarded and made strong and fruitful; those that would not they drove to the far places. They invoked their ancient compacts with the royalty of the beasts they had preserved from the otherworld and married them to the princes of the beasts of the land the ship had found, and in presiding over such unions brought harmony to the world and made it a place fit to be ruled by men.

But the ancients foresaw that their age of greatness was fading. This was the Elder age, when monsters did the will of men to build great things and ships sailed on the sea of night. The ancients knew that their time of power was com-

ever. But there was economic collapse back home, caused in no small part by the vast resource-sink of the colonising initiative, and the colonies were mostly still at a state where they had been expecting further shipments of people and technology in order to maintain their standards of living. However, being colonists, they adapted to what they had. They did their best to set up stable living systems that would ensure food and health for their descendants, and probably they watched the skies and hoped that Earth would come through for them. And, as the generations came and went, they forgot their science piece by piece, and could not mend what broke down. Their ancestors had done well in giving them life on an alien world, but they forgot that was what they lived on, and

ing to an end, and taught such lore as they could to those who would come after. The ancients told that the pale harbours of the otherworld sat empty, and none put out from their docks anymore. No sails were on the sea of night and the servants of the ancients grew unruly and rebellious, and had to be destroyed or driven to the far places. The ancients retreated to their places and knew that their time in the world was done. Some yet watched the night sky, but there were no more travellers from the otherworld. Some allowed their magic to dwindle and became like other men, and others fled back to the otherworld rather than face that fate. Some closed the doors of their tombs and were seen no more. And their descendants lived without magic, but farmed the land and traded and built. And

where they had come from, and just concentrated on surviving and prospering without the tools they no longer had, and the knowledge that was no longer of any use. if they laid stone on stone without the help of the ancients' marvellous servants, and without understanding of the ancients' magics, yet they lived and prospered.

Nyr

AND WHEN I'VE SAID all that, when I've committed that unconscionable betrayal of all the non-contamination rules they pounded into me at anthropology HQ, the two women just look at me, and Lyn says, "Yes, that is how we tell it." They look at me quite blankly, no idea how what I've just said connects to what I was saying before, my ridiculous little outburst. I almost stamp my foot in frustration. I have just told them that their whole culture is a lie, basically, a ridiculous fake thing that grew out of a failed colony that lost its way, and they nod and say, "Well, yes, of course."

"There are no demons, no magic," I say, but only weakly. The two women regard me as though I'm supposed to do a trick now, pull an animal out of my ear, guess the number they're thinking of.

Worst of both worlds, really. I've just had a bit of a meltdown, to be honest. The DCS was already fragile, and when Lyn was making all those promises in my name, to all those wretched, filthy, desperate people, there was a moment of utter synchronicity between the buried feelings it was keeping down and my higher brain, all of me thinking, *This is wrong,* and so when we got back here I let it all off the leash and railed at them, as profoundly unprofessional as you can get, not a note taken, not a folkway recorded for posterity. I told them their culture is bunk, based on ludicrous fabrications about how things are and how it'll all work out, just the way an anthropologist should never do. And then, with my professional integrity in tatters, they didn't actually understand what I was saying. Somehow I told them something else instead.

I reboot the DCS and feel a great deal better, while knowing that such feeling is itself illusory, and in reality I feel very bad indeed.

"So, we'll go and find where this demon is, then," I say calmly. And perhaps it will be interesting. Perhaps it will make a nice footnote to one of my reports, that I can send off into the void in the general manner of a man hurling curses at the thunder. Doubtless, despite the prolonged lack of any contact from Earth, they're all eagerly awaiting my next bulletin.

"Thank you, Nyrgoth Elder. Nyr."

I blink. Lyn is kneeling in front of me, almost touching my knee but pulling back, that reluctance they have towards any physical intimacy. Something of my puzzlement must have shown on my face, because she draws back and stands up hurriedly, just before I think about reaching forward myself, closing that circuit between us. Most likely for the best.

"Our ship was very small, that carried us here," I tell her, speaking as precisely as I can. For some reason it is important that I make her understand this one thing. "When my fellow scientists and I travelled from Earth to your world, we were all at each other's elbows and knees, like too many eating at a small table. Unlike your ancestors, we had star drives that were very small even though they harnessed powers that were very mighty." And who knows what she makes of any of that, given the approximations and guesses I have to make, in the translation. "Back in the world I came from, too, those parts of it that are habitable are crowded, all of us living in each other's pockets, on all sides, above and below. For someone to lay their hand on your shoulder or move you to one side or clasp your arm in greeting, that happened a hundred times in a day. Even out in the camp beyond these walls, they have more room each than any of us dreamt of. And it was the same for your ancestors before they set off, or why else travel so far to find a new home?"

Lyn regards me, and I know I have got it wrong again. She is trying to hide it, but I can see she has heard something else. Perhaps I have told her of the conditions of damned souls in hell. Behind the gates of the DCS my mood sinks even further, but on the surface I am san-guine. I make another note for the study.

———————

In the morning we are joined by the one-handed man, Allwerith. From past observation I am aware that his mu-tilation was part of the judicial process he described, and that under other circumstances such a man would be dri-ven from the sight of Watacha's walls, or any civilized place, given no option but to be a wildman or a brigand. However, Lyn looks him up and down as he stands there in his ragged clothes, and greets him with a wary respect, using a register that signifies higher speaking to lower, but not highest to lowest as she would be entitled to use. I have heard her discussing the man with Esha, and his presence here, rather than, say, on the roads preying on the refugees, has impressed her.

"What was your crime?" she asks.

Allwerith flinches but faces up to her. "Theft, more than once. And I won't tell you of starving children or the like. I stole precious things because I didn't have them and others did. I won't make it out to be a noble busi-ness."

"Will you take us towards Farbourand and the de-mon?"

A muscle tics in his jaw. "Lynesse Fourth Daughter of Lannesite, you ask much of a poor man."

"I ask much of a bold man, even if he was once a thief. Did you steal in Farbourand?"

"Less than most."

"Then serve me in this, and I shall vouch for you, and so shall Jerevesse Third Daughter. You shall have a pardon and a station."

I consider that he will not get his fingers back, and for a moment I almost promise him that as well, because if I can get him back to the outpost then the medical facilities there could grow fresh tissue from the stumps. I have been sufficiently unprofessional already, and I cannot face the looks on their faces as they mouth *Magic* to each other, and so I say nothing.

But fingers or not, there are tears in Allwerith's eyes. The very permanency of his punishment shows that men such as he are condemned forever without any prospect of rehabilitation. What Lyn has promised him is more than he could ever have hoped for.

I speak with him later. He is plainly in awe of me, even though I am doing absolutely nothing to foster anybody's delusions. The horns, alas, do not help. I ask him about this "demon" and how it manifests. Has he ever seen the thing itself? He saw something, his cords and circles and whatnot, but he thought perhaps it was the demon's house, or a gate to the world where demons dwell. He saw neither man nor monster that might have been the demon in the flesh, only those unfortunates turned into its servants. How did he know those servants? The mark of the demon was on them, eyes and crystals and stuff like rot on a tree—which in this world means scaly growths like flaking eczema or peeling sunburn. He claimed they acted all together, people and animals, in attacking settlements, so he knew that a demon moved them all.

Possibly it is some mind-affecting poison, something like the ergot that once grew on wheat. I may be able to send back to the outpost via the satellite, for a rudimentary chemical analysis. Perhaps that will lead to a cure, or at least some vaccination to stop the business spreading. I may yet be able to do some good, even though I am no magician and there is no demon to be slain.

I show Allwerith the claw that Esha obtained, and he confirms with a flinch that, yes, it is a thing of the demon. The base material is the mandible of a shreeling, which are common around Farbourand, but the greenish-black encrustations are the demon's mark. The next night, some way west of Watacha as we camp, I do my best to dissect the nasty little thing and find some organic material under the scales and plates of the infection. There seems to be nothing, though. I force my eyes to a higher magnification than their specifications recommend, and find no internal structure in any of it, just solid pieces as though the whole mess had been glued onto the mandible as a practical joke or a bizarre craft activity. None of this is exactly something I was trained in, anthropologist second class as I am, and eventually I give up on it. A living specimen will obviously be necessary to get anywhere.

Two more days of good progress through the forest; little conversation; Esha and Allwerith—no, Allwer the others call him now, which I think is an indication of his changed status—ranging ahead much of the time. We came near two small communities of forest people, both nominally within the fiefdom of Watacha. The first was on high alert, with archers and spears at the palisade wall. The people there said they had seen sign of the demon's creatures in the trees. I expected Lyn to tell them the same line about bringing her magician to fight the demon, but she glanced at me and simply said we were here to see what we could do. I fear that many of the watchers saw me and drew their own conclusions anyway, but at least I was not knowingly being oversold.

The second community we came to was abandoned,

though there was no sign of violence nor of any evident in-fection. The locals had obviously gone to that large camp about Watacha. Or else, as per Allwer's cheer-inspiring sug-gestion, the demon had simply taken them all, all at once and without the chance to fight.

I ask him questions to try to determine a kind of vector of infection, in case we are dealing with some novel plague. How does this "demon" select and take over its victims? All-wer says many of those who went close to the demon's place near Farbourand were chosen, as were others who had been injured by demon-tainted fauna and flora. But some simply fell to it, exhibiting the marks of its influence without obvi-ous prequel. Similarly, others had exposure but never took up the infection, including Allwer himself. I take the liberty of extracting a sample of his blood, which he is unhappy about but too wary of supposed magical retribution to refuse. It is possible that he has a resistance that can be spread through the population. Again, I lack the tools, but I send information to the satellite and await more data.

The same day we passed the empty settlement, we see the mark of the demon.

There is a kind of creature the locals call a vermid, which is a direct descendant of the old Earth English word "vermin" and suggests that they were an unin-tended escapee from the early colonial breeding pro-gramme. They are augmented rodent stock, very at home in trees, about half the length of a human arm plus twice that in prehensile tail. Their mélange of artificial, Earth and native biochemistry makes them voraciously omnivorous, a pest in multiple ways.

There are worse plagues than vermids, as we find. We come across some that carry the "demon" infection and it is a profoundly disquieting sight. They are certainly sick with something, and I am immediately put into mind of parasitic Earth fungi whose life cycle involves making profound behavioural and physiological changes to their hosts.

The vermids are all together in a kind of a spire. I count twenty-seven of them, but I may be mistaken because they are partially merged together into a single living mass, limbs, heads, tails all fused at various points to make a single body at least four metres tall. We see individuals, or parts of individuals, moving, though more so towards the structure's tip; the lower members, partially fused into some root system below, are still. The whole is mottled over with patches of the infection, eruptions of chitinous-looking pustules and little nests of beads like black eyes, odd stiff fibres or hairs, patches of scaly hide as though the vermids had been the victims of some inconclusive transformation into some other, even less savoury, creature.

I tell the others to stay back and receive no arguments.

I approach only with caution myself, setting my immune system on high alert to repel anything even vaguely inimical to my system. I start feeling hot and uncomfortable immediately, but that's just telling me my precautions are active. Everything will bring me out in a rash right now, but I hope that will also let me fight off any pathogen that tries it on with me.

I sample some of the vermid-thing, cutting a twitching toe off one luckless beast and then stepping back in case the whole decides to retaliate. No response from it, whatever it is. My best bet is some kind of fruiting body, like a mushroom, which presupposes that the infection distributes itself via airborne spores.

Except my other internal instruments are picking up curious trace signals There are electromagnetic fluctuations about the grotesque spire that are definitely not present in the wider forest. They go ... nowhere I can tell. Another step back and they are no longer detectable, from present to absent without any moment when they are simply *less*. Measuring a wide spectrum in the spire's vicinity, I find a series of wavelengths in use, some a little past the infrared range, some in the spectrum used for shortwave radio communications, others around the level of X-rays. It's all so scattershot that I likely wouldn't have picked up on it save that there is a rhythm to the activity, not simultaneously on all bands but passed from one to another. A rhythm that lacks regularity, but which has repeated sections, almost a call and response, that I can track from wavelength to wavelength. The signals are not strong, and the radiation is less dangerous than direct sunlight. They seem to be in dialogue with something, but they are undetectable just a few metres from source. Which I cannot account for. It's as though they're vanishing into a hole, or I'm detecting them as bouceback from somewhere, via some atmospheric trick.

My analysis of the vermid toe, that night, reveals no unusual microbial life within it, neither Earth-style nor the simpler local analogues, nor the engineered hybrids of the two that the colonists worked up.

I find nothing that accounts for the odd electromagnetic activity.

We leave the vermids behind, heading for Birchari, which Allwer says was taken by the infection only ten days ago. I don't believe in demons, but given what we've seen, I don't blame these people for using the word.

Lynesse

LYN HAD GOT HERSELF out of sight of the others before losing her breakfast. One more reason to envy the sorcerer his ability to set aside his emotions until some more convenient time. She had heard the tales, but tales are exaggerated in the telling, everyone knew. Except this was worse than anyone had said, as though the demon had spent the intervening time devising new amusements for itself.

It was not the plight of the vermids themselves that had overthrown her stomach, but the thought that, somewhere in the forest, there might be a similar spire twenty feet tall and built of writhing human beings, fused together in the same abominable way.

Esha woke her halfway through that night, a hand to her shoulder and an urgent murmur in her ear. She clutched for her sword, envisaging . . . Except the horrors she could imagine surely paled compared to what was actually out there. But there was *something* out there, Esh' said. Something large, but being quiet. Not a comforting combination.

They woke the others, even Nyrgoth Elder. Weapons to hand they stalked through the midnight woods, jumping at every cracked twig, backing into one another, their hoarse and frightened breath jagged in one another's ears. Lyn saw the thing move ahead, a great angular mound of a creature squatting over the rotted bole of a fallen tree. For a long time it was no more than a shadow, shifting position occasionally on its many legs. Then . . .

"It's the wizard's monster," Esha said. Her eyes were better in the dark. Allwer, of course, was leery enough about a wizard, let alone any attendant familiar, and had to have the story recounted to him. The thing that had devoured Lyn's sword back near the Elder's tower.

Nyrgoth just stared at them blankly. "Where is the demon?" he asked, obviously expecting a continuation of their hunt. Because, apparently, he'd known the monster was here all along, as they stealthily crept up on it. He just hadn't thought to mention it.

"It won't harm us," he told them, still not really understanding. "It hears my voice. I am most of what it can hear in the world, and so it follows me. But it will not break my forbiddances. Soon, most likely, some part of it will fail and we will leave it behind."

Perhaps it was the monster's reappearance and ready dismissal that left them unprepared for what they found next.

Allwer had led them to the walls of Birchari, a town only nominally within Watacha's curtilage, practically self-governing save when the tax caravan came. There would be no levies anymore. Half the place was a fire-scar that must have been fed with oil and the aromatic sap that the Ord fiefdoms exported, that smelled so good and burned so fiercely. The scent was heavy across the air, and probably it masked less wholesome odours. The fire had scorched across the buildings, the wooden wall and a swath of the forest itself before dying out. There were plenty of charred bodies, men and beasts both.

"No demon work this?" Esha asked hollowly.

"I'd say not," was Allwer's sober reply. "But they set the fires because of it."

Having seen what the demon could do, Lyn reckoned burning was the more merciful fate.

"How did it get past the walls?" she pressed.

"It was already within the walls, within the people," Allwer said.

"Do we go in?" Esha was obviously not keen.

"I will need to study its sign further," Nyrgoth Elder said, and Lyn wanted to go, too.

"We are going on to Farbourand, or as close as we can, to the house of the demon that Allwer saw. Do you think anything we see in Birchari's ruins will be worse than that? Let us see what can be seen. Let us grow strong from viewing its crimes, and teach ourselves vengeance."

"Fine words," Esha said tiredly, because she had heard that epic poem, too, and had little time for it. Lyn was primarily trying to kindle courage within herself, though. The rest could take or leave the heroic sagas, but the tales had been her inspiration when she was a child and they had carried her to the Tower of the Elders. She could only hope they'd take her farther still.

She drew her sword and Esha followed suit, cupping a sling in her off-hand, lead bullet palmed and ready. All-wer had a stout cudgel, and likely his exile had taught him how to use it.

They padded cautiously in through the great black-ened gap in the walls the fire had made, seeing the logs splintered outwards where barrels of sap had exploded in the heat. The intact buildings beyond bore mottled patches of scaly rot, many of them trailing long whiskers that twitched and swayed where there was no wind, winking with black beads that Lyn could only think of as eyes. *Which means the demon sees us.*

Nyrgoth Elder was stepping towards the closest stand-ing wall, already with some of his little metal tools in hand, just as he had carved off and sealed away a piece of the vermid spire. Lyn kept close behind him, holding her sword high so the demon could see just how much she wasn't scared of it.

Something moved between the buildings and she let out a startled hiss and stepped back, freezing the rest in their tracks.

"I saw someone," she swore.

"Someone, or a dead-thing?" Esha demanded, a single suffix turning the word from meaning a living beast to something sick, dead or rotten; unclean.

"It walked like a person," Lyn hazarded, and then further explanation was unnecessary, for it—they—came limping out.

She counted three of them. Only one had been human. Of the others, one was a cerkitt, a long-bodied, short-limbed beast the Bircharii had kept for hunting. It still had its collar, although the flesh of its neck was puffed out in bulbous blisters so that the strap was almost lost within. One side of its body had moulted its feathery pelt, revealing a hide erupting with sores and more of those hard black eyes. The second non-human figure was made of sarkers, a pest from here all the way to Lannesite. Lyn knew the hand-sized six-legged creatures because there was a bounty on them each Storm-season's End and people queued up at her mother's palace to claim the reward, sticks over their shoulders from which the little bodies swung. At first she thought she was seeing a malformed sarker the size of a man, lurching along on oddly joined legs, but then she realised she was seeing a sarker *made* of sarkers, a hundred of the beasts just mashed together into the right general shape, lumpen body, twisted limbs, but all of it made from still-living animals whose free limbs and mouth parts writhed in constant agony.

Between these two prodigies was something that had been a man, once. He stood on two legs, profoundly lopsided. He still wore a forester's hard-wearing clothes, though the seams had ripped down one side to the waist where his back and shoulder had bloated out with hard plates and jags, between which protruded long frilled filaments. On his other shoulder was an extra arm and part of a head, as though someone had been huddling close to him and then most of her had been taken away, leaving only those parts. The single remaining eye was closed, and Lyn was thankful. His own head, canted at an odd angle, was three-quarters obscured by a thick growth of the demon-mark, including both eye sockets. Five gleaming discs winked at them from within the shaggy mass.

"Ancestors preserve us," Esha said frankly. "Let's get out of here."

"No," Lyn said, because if they left now, they'd never stop running until they got to Lannesite, and then where would she be? And where would Watacha be? And how long before the demon spread its corruption across the Barrenpike and into her homeland?

And Nyrgoth said, "There is a voice."

There was no voice anyone else could hear, and the three monstrosities were still lurching forwards, impeded by their own mutations. Nyrgoth did seem to be concentrating, though. He had a hand up and cast it about, as though it was some new form of ear he could use to track down what he heard.

"Within them, and within all the patches of sickness," he said. "There is a voice that speaks, all to the same rhythm. And it speaks to . . . elsewhere. It calls elsewhere and hears commands, but I cannot tell how the voice is brought here or how it leaves. Most curious."

"I hear no voice," Lyn said. The things were getting close and she wanted to pluck at the sorcerer's sleeve.

"You wouldn't. It is not a voice made by the throat, but I hear it still. And I can speak in that same register."

"You can *talk* to these things? Or to the demon, through them?" Esha asked him incredulously. "Can you banish it?"

"I don't know. And I don't think there is anything to talk to, not an intelligence. But if this voice is a part of its life, that binds its parts together, perhaps I can use a like voice to break it apart." He sounded absurdly calm in the face of the oncoming horrors, and Lyn felt her own nerves grate between her teeth and on the inside of her skull. She could not stand this much longer. She could not maintain a hero's proper reserve.

"Do it!" she told him.

"Yes, well," he said, and the three things stopped and shivered abruptly. There were not even words of command or magic gestures, simply the will of the magician holding them in thrall.

Allwer let out a long, tattered breath. He was behind Esha, Lyn saw, but he hadn't run and his cudgel was at the ready, which spoke well for her trust of him.

"Have you mastered them?" she asked.

"Not so much." Nyrgoth was frowning. "I am shouting over the voice it uses between its different parts, so it cannot hear itself. And, not hearing its own commands, these parts of it stand idle...." His eyes narrowed. "It speaks."

"You said that."

Nyrgoth Elder was very still. "It speaks to me."

Lyn felt physically sick. "You are a sorcerer. You can resist it."

"Not like that." Horror did not move him, but some dire revelation had plainly touched him. "It is aware of me, I have spoken as it speaks. And so it questions me. I don't understand. What have we met here?"

"What does it ask?" Lyn could not push past a whisper.

"Nothing, no words I know, but I'd guess it wants to

know what I am. I think I'm probably the first thing it's met here that is real to it."

"The people of Farbourand, of this place," Allwer pressed.

"A resource." The coolness of his voice was almost as dreadful as the demon-slaves before them. "Your demon does not hear human words. Perhaps does not exist as a material being at all. But it exists in the speech it uses, between its parts, and now so do I." A change in tone as he considered. "So what *are* you, precisely . . . ?"

The monsters all jerked at the same time, puppets sharing strings. Lyn saw their limbs twist in ways that must have torn up the tissues of their joints.

"I think I have an understanding," Nyrgoth said lightly. "Not what it is, but how it works, at least. I can create a region that will exclude the demon's voice. Which will hopefully protect us from falling prey to the thing ourselves." He glanced at her and there was even a small smile on his face, as though the whole hideous business had just been a word puzzle posed to the company over supper.

"Watch!" Esha yelled, right on the heels of his words, and then the Coast-woman lunged in, yanking Lyn back hard enough to spill her on the ground. Nyrgoth Elder whirled round, focused more on Esha than the monsters, and something unfolded out of the corrupted man's chest: a barbed, four-jointed arm that must have filled most of his chest cavity. It snapped forwards, farther than a spearman could have lunged, and drove itself into Nyrgoth's gut in a spray of blood.

Nyr

ow.
   bloody
   stabbed me.

———————

The problem with pain is that
   while it is in theory a good warning light on the control panel of the mind to warn you to take your hand out
of the fire—
   it's—
   just—
   that—

———————

When all the lights go on like a fireworks display they get
in the way of pressing the right buttons.

———————

Which is why I have the option of
　　turning it off,
　　transmuting all those
　　irritating
　　attempts at the body to save itself into
　　calm little reports and readouts and memos from my
internal systems.
　　but
　　when things get to this state
　　(*when some infected bloody monster shoves its fucking
ovipositor into my stomach*)
　　the stately march of little reports becomes a blizzard
of warnings and error messages, until I cannot *see*. Until
sensory information from my actual senses has been entirely shunted out of the way by my rich internal techni-
cal life insisting that I click through all the windows and
menus. I'd take it up with the manufacturers if that were
in any way a realistic proposition.

　　And you know how it is when you've got some device
on which you depend for all manner of little tasks that,
perhaps, once you could have done without but which is
now entirely essential to your well-being. You know how
it is when that starts to go wrong, throws up its warning
signs, groans and shudders, slows down, won't start? The
sense of aggrieved helplessness that, oh no, I'm going to
have to get this *fixed* now, or I won't be able to do all the

stuff I need to get done. That sense of sick, yawning horror because, despite you being such a civilized sophisticate, you don't really understand how any of it works to the extent that it might as well be magic? Well, that, basically, except the computer is you, the warning signs and fatal exception errors are you, and if it shuts down and won't reboot then that's all she wrote.

And so here I am, just getting rid of the errors, just swiping them off to the left side of my mind's eye, trying to get to a point where I'm in at least nominal control of my own mind. And I almost miss the big one. Really, they should have made it twice the size of the rest.

Final warning: Ultimate Anti-contamination Measures activated.

I almost just swipe it, because I'm still panicking, in a frenzy of *Just get out of the way* with all these sleeting cautions and messages my system's throwing up. I realise what it actually means just in time.

Countermand! I tell it inside my head. *Countermand Ultimate Anti-contamination Measures! Acknowledge. I'm not dead! I am not fucking dead!*

I think I'm too late, for a second. Warnings are still coming down fast and hard, and the mulish little acknowledgement is nearly lost in the chaos. Up above, I imagine the satellite cruising the heavens, already warmed up and ready to fulfil its most extreme function to preserve the integrity of the culture under study. Because all those rules I'm so cavalier about, the ones I've broken far too often and am breaking right now by getting involved, they were supposed to be of supreme importance. No point studying the culture if it gets hold of our stuff and suddenly leaps out of barbarism and into the space age, after all. Where's the fun in that?

That done, I deal with the rest of the stuff. I reinstall the DCS and get it going again, which means I am immediately better suited to actually respond to the rest of it. I boil down the medical information to something I can digest. Healing procedures are in place. Tissue is regenerating. Considerable damage to several important organs, but I am augmented sufficiently that I could probably take out my own heart and mend it by hand if I had to, so long as I was done within an hour or two. I am going to pull through.

I don't already know how long it's been, because system feedback wiped out my internal continuity, but the satellite claims almost two hours have passed since the stabbing. Unless my assailant is taking a really leisurely time about it, I'm unlikely to be stabbed again. Have I been compromised by the infection? Waking up to find myself part of a permanent human pyramid might make me regret I turned down the Ultimate, because it's not a system I can just activate on a whim.

No, I had formulated my defences and they were in place before the attempted evisceration.

I open my eyes.

We are in a forest clearing. They've laid me beside a fallen tree with a blanket under me and another one over, and they're askew, which suggests Lyn because Esha is very neat in her placement of everything.

Can I sit up? I consult my inner doctor. The tissue regeneration is advanced enough that gentle activity is permitted. I sit up.

Someone screams from right next to me, sending a clench of shock through muscles that really could have done without the exercise. Allwerith—no, Allwer, sorry—has leapt to his feet. Apparently, it was his turn to sit with the dying wizard. Or possibly the dead wizard. I realise belatedly that the blanket being over my face probably had certain cultural implications. Another failure of anthropology.

"Well, that's why I'm only second class," I say, which wouldn't mean anything to them even if I said it in their language.

I look across the clearing and see Lyn.

She has changed clothes. She'd come all this way wearing drab and hard-wearing stuff, animal hide and heavy fabric, the sort of thing you'd want to tramp about the countryside in if you didn't have my advantages. Now she's wearing something much finer: a cuirass (is that the word?) of metal scales that must have been rolled up at the bottom of her pack, and under it a magnificently embroidered blouse, black shot through with silver thread. On the shoulders, where the mission insignia would have been on an old colonial uniform, are red blazons showing a spread-winged emblem that can trace its pictographic lineage to the old landing craft that came down just about where the Lanessite palace now stands. She has a little shield rattling about, grip looped over the hilt of her sheathed sword. She is every inch the warrior princess and, even in my current sorry state, I am embarrassed to say that my heart skips a beat.

She looks so much like Astresse. Her ancestor went to war in rather more metal, true, but the colours are the same, and so is the stance. Someone who is going to pick a fight with a demon, a sorcerer, a monster, something superhuman they cannot understand but know they must oppose.

"Are you . . . you?" she asks, and I realise that a hand close to her sword hilt is not just posturing.

"I am not infected." Although I am less sure now that "infected" is even the right word. "I am proof against it."

Her eyes are red. Surely not weeping for me. With the cool rationality imposed by the DCS I confirm that, no, not for me, because if it had been then she'd look a bit more cheerful now I'm walking and talking. Allwer is right here, which means . . .

"Esha has it," she says bleakly. "When the demon-slaves attacked, you destroyed the one that struck you with fire, and we fell on the others, all three of us, and hacked and beat them till they were nothing. But after we carried your body—carried *you*—from Birchari, she . . . the mark appeared on her."

"Help me up, please. Take me to her."

Allwer lends me his arm, the one without fingers at the end of it, and I can get myself to my feet with only a little leaning on him. His eyes are very wide, at least half as scared of me as he is of the demon. Putting one foot in front of another is still something of a complex piece of logistics, and every step throws up a few more laggard error messages I have to deal with, but he gets me over to where Esha is lying.

She is still herself. Her face is full of the awareness of what is happening to her. The scaly stuff is growing on one side of her head and there are patches of raw skin there where someone tried to just abrade it away until she bled, only to find that it sprouted from the wounds just as readily. A few of those glinting black beads are scattered along the line of her cheekbone. Sense organs, but not actually eyes, I think. I am wondering if the controlling force actually perceives the physical world as we do, even vicariously through its minions.

My systems throw up another gout of errors, like a half-drowned man coughing up the last lungful of water, then start doing their job. I can detect that electromagnetic signature, just like before. It comes from nowhere, goes nowhere. If I step back there is no sign of it, impossible to intercept, just ... *there* at the point of infection. Like hearing the sound from an open door as you pass it. My mind hooks on to that idea. *An open door ... to where, though?* And this is impossible. This is not how the electromagnetic spectrum *works*. You can't just have a signal that appears at its destination point without travelling through the intervening space from its origination. I don't know what we're dealing with here.

But I know about how it does what it does. I kneel by Esha, seeing her eyes track me. Tears trickle down her cheek, and I see a whip-like filament grope towards them from the scabbed infection.

"Do it," she gets out. "I asked Lynesse, but she wouldn't. But you will, won't you? You don't feel like we feel. You can't regret."

"I will later," I tell her. "There are a great many things I will regret later, and perhaps forever. But right now I don't have to feel."

"Then do it, please," she says, and closes her eyes hard, gritting her teeth.

I do it. I extend the field my systems generate until it encompasses her.

A ripple passes across the patch of corruption growing on her, and I see dozens of hair-thin arms stretch from between the scales and wave about blindly as though reaching for something. I get my instruments out, but I fear my hands are not going to be steady enough for the work. I have limited reserves of physical energy, given the prodigious self-repair efforts currently underway.

"Lyn, Allwer, come here." I give them my multitool, demonstrating how it can be adjusted from one shape to another, a task they pick up more swiftly than I did the first time I had to use it. "Remove the infestation from her, as carefully as you can."

It comes off more easily than I'd thought, and I think that I am interfering not just with the communications signal but also with some interaction between the parasite and its substrate. Even so, it is an hour's hard work to pry everything off Esha's face, and then attend to the other patches of it on her body, that I can track down from its frustrated attempts to reconnect. Esha will bear the scars forever, more from the removal than the actual infection, but I honestly don't think she'll care.

In the end I let down the field again and wait to see if I detect any of the demon's ethereal chatter. Only silence, blessed silence. I pronounce her cured, and then reinstate the field strongly enough to cover all four of us, setting up a battery of subsystems to maintain it no matter what.

I'm very tired, after that, and sit down on the blanket, back against the fallen tree. There is a long silence, and eventually I open my eyes to find all three of them staring at me.

"What?" I ask, somewhat irritably.

"I owe you my life," says Esha simply. "I need to repay that debt. How does one do that, with one such as you?" Almost peevish. Because, in saving her, I've cut through all manner of traditions that are trying to reattach around the mess I've made, just like the demon-infection. And, because I'm *not* a part of their world, their ways can't accommodate me and there will be a social scar forever from my meddling.

"Just . . . I've done too much already, interfered too much. Just . . . say thanks, or something." I wave a hand vaguely.

"I will find a way," Esha insists. I can see it's going to eat at her. Better that than other things.

"If you were a chirurgeon, I would give you honours in my mother's name, patronage, property," Lyn says. "You saved my closest friend." As Esha's patron she's equally bound, and equally awkward.

"Look, Lyn," and again that flinch, and on the back

of my musing I realise why. We are not friends, and I've been taking liberties without realising. "Lynesse Fourth Daughter," I tell her formally, "I am going to tell you something else that I have no proper words for in this language. I was sent to watch your people, and see how you lived, so that my people could learn about you. Sent by my people, who are long gone now, so that I may as well be the last of the Elder Race, as you call me. I was sent to watch and not act. To watch you sicken, to watch you make war; to watch you die so that I could learn your funerary practices. To watch and never interfere, in case I contaminated you with my own superior culture. And I bent the rules a bit, when you had problems that originated with relics from older days. I told myself it wasn't really contamination when I was removing other outside influences. I was very good at weaselling out of the rules." And all put into her language as best I can, and have I communicated the precise connotations of "weaselling" to someone who doesn't know what a weasel is? "And now I've taken matters entirely too far. You couldn't know, but the greatest danger you were ever in just now came from *me*, because if I had died, or even if it appeared that I was going to die, then . . ." And how do I tell her about the satellite in its eternal orbit out beyond the edge of the atmosphere? "Then fire from heaven, Lynesse. Just to stop you getting hold of my body." She doesn't understand, but that's probably for the best. I am only now, at the wrong end of three centuries after loss of contact, beginning to realise just how broken my own *superior* culture actually was. They set us here to make exhaustive anthropological notes on the fall of every sparrow. But not to catch a single one of them. To *know*, but very emphatically not to *care*.

Lyn kneels down beside me, though still with a definite distance. "You have earned the right to call me Lyn, if you wish." It is a huge concession and one that she is frightened about making. I search my records and recollections, and I guess that in normal social situations this would be an open door to greater intimacy in the future, letting me across some invisible but crucial threshold. And she is scared of me and what I might do without that door between us, and I can't honestly say that she is wrong to be, because I am a *mess*, and when the DCS lifts, who knows what I'll feel? Not to mention that getting on the equivalent of first-name terms with one of the locals is also absolutely against contamination procedures. And so obviously I should say no. That would be the rational DCS-prompted choice.

But the word doesn't actually come out, and I nod instead and say nothing, and apparently that is acceptance enough, because an extra spark of fear lights in her eyes and stays there. She is the princess from the stories who has made a promise to a wizard, and knows that it will be collected on. And I am that wizard, and don't know what I might do when I am not (or when I am more) myself.

What I actually say is, "Why are you dressed like that, anyway?"

The non sequitur catches her by surprise and she looks abruptly defensive and embarrassed. "You were dead," she tells me. "Esha was sick. I was going to have Allwer lead me to the demon's house beyond Farbourand. And call it out."

"You were going to do what?" I honestly do not understand what she means.

"I was going to call it out. Challenge the demon to fight me," she says defiantly, and then, her voice breaking with the sheer desperation of it all, "It's how it's done."

Something is building up inside me, behind the shield of the DCS. I see it approach as one might dispassionately watch a flash flood while standing in the dry riverbed. Of course, the DCS will keep it all bottled up so I can make safely reasonable decisions. No matter that all my systems are stretched to the limit with the self-repair effort. No matter that I've been leaning on it far too much since my outburst at Watacha.

I feel my heart break, in a way that I would never be able to fix, not even if I took it out right now and tinkered with it. Staring at Lynesse Fourth Daughter, dressed in her finest, sword at her hip, off to do something that is *What Princesses Do* when there are monsters and demons and wizards in the world. Something that was surely not actually what they did, back in the days her myth-cycles originated in. Because myths miss out all the sordid realities and preserve only *What we wish we'd done,* rather than *How we actually did it.* But she's brave, and maybe she's stupid, and she knows that this thing, that even I don't understand, needs to be faced down and defeated, and she doesn't know any other way. And, frankly, there is probably no response available to her culture and available technology that would be any better, so: Single combat, why not?

I am overwhelmed by a terrible sadness, but it's a good sadness in a way. It isn't the leaden weight of my own self-pity and misery, the biochemical fallout of malfunctioning metabolism and cognition that just casts a dour filter over everything, whether there's cause or not. I am sad for Lynesse Fourth Daughter, trying to be something that never existed in the world, and failing because it's impossible, and trying again.

"Let us go to Farbourand and the demon's house," I tell her. "I don't know what we will find there or what we can do about it, but I can keep the demon from placing its mark on us. I'd rather we avoided the mobile elements of the demon because, as you've seen, I can't ward off physical harm as I can its influence. But if we can get to this origin point then . . . who knows?"

I look at the other two. Neither of them wants to do this, and I'd not blame them for leaving. Esha loves Lyn, though, and would not leave her, and Allwer . . . something of Lyn's fire has kindled in him, I think. He is a man who has made bad choices and suffered for them, and had written his own life off as lost. Now he has the chance to remake himself and, having cut away all that bad history, we find a strength of character underneath that even he would not have guessed at.

"I'll lead you there," he confirms, looking as though he can't believe what he's saying. "I'll show you the demon."

Lynesse

THE NEXT NIGHT, NYRGOTH Elder insisted they find a clearing, and then spent some time staring blankly at the clear night sky, at the frost-glints of stars. Sitting unobtrusively close, Lyn saw his lips move, an inaudible conversation with an invisible presence. He finished abruptly, turning right into her attention so she had no time to pretend she had been doing anything else but watching him.

"I'm . . . speaking with my familiar," he told her, "as if that would mean anything to you."

It was by no means the strangest thing he had said. She knew the word well from the palace, where it covered a variety of hangers-on, servants and courtiers who moved about their greaters in respectful dances.

"Another worker?" Using the archaic word he'd chosen when speaking of the beast they'd met in the mountains.

"Although sometimes my master, also," he agreed, and that also seemed entirely in keeping with what she knew of wizards from the stories. "It passed over us, and I have seen what it saw. The forest covers much, but I see Farbourand, and I see beyond to where this thing is, whatever it is. My familiar sees a structure of some kind there, that must be what Allwer saw. You couldn't miss it from Farbourand's walls now."

"And Farbourand itself?"

"Overgrown. Not by the forest but by . . . the usual. We don't want to go there."

"Your familiar, can it do anything else except look?" Because she wasn't going to turn away any help, right now.

He blinked, and she sensed he was puzzled, though if so it was a puzzlement locked deep within him, only a faint curiosity making it to his face. "It can do many things, but it won't. I do not have the authority to simply make it obey. There are rules governing what it will do at my bidding, and what it will do of its own reckoning. Lyn . . . esse Fourth Daughter, forgive me, but you are taking what I say very calmly. You . . . I'm sorry, you can't understand what I . . ." He frowned. "And I shouldn't tell you, of course." Sorcerers were reticent creatures, after all. Perhaps part of his bargain with the familiar was that he kept its secrets.

"Can you at least tell me what the demon said to you?" she asked. The attack, Esha's infection, these things had shouted louder than his revelation just before, but she had been given plenty of time to brood. "Did it tell you what it wanted? Is there some way we can command it, or placate it?" She had been very ready to fight the demon, but the more she had girded on her armour and readied herself to make her challenge, the less she felt it would achieve. A late moment to start thinking like her mother, that grand storybook gestures were perhaps not the most efficacious way to help the world.

Nyrgoth Elder was staring blankly at her, but then he plainly understood what she meant. "It spoke," he said slowly. "I could not understand it. Whatever it said to me was different from the communion it had with the parts of itself. But . . ." He shook his head. "I don't have the language, in my tongue or yours. It wants something. Or at least it is driven to do something, perhaps, from its very nature, as a tree's nature is to grow. Not conquest. Not hunger. Not cruelty. It has a need and a reason for doing what it does and being as it is. But neither need nor reason meant anything to me. I don't even have words or concepts for it." The thought seemed to badly shake him, and she felt as though the ground itself had become unstable beneath her. This was the Elder, the ancient sorcerer who had lived in his impregnable tower since the dawn of time and come back from the dead. And he *feared*, even if it was his lack of understanding he feared more than the demon itself.

"You use this word, 'demon,'" he said at last. "What do you even mean by it?"

Lyn frowned at him. It hardly seemed her place to lesson a sorcerer in such things. "Surely you . . ."

"You remember the broken worker we met in the mountains?"

"That yet follows you."

"I've told it to sleep, to go away, but the part of it that should obey such words is flawed." He shrugged. "You wouldn't call it a 'demon'?"

"No." Obviously, but apparently not to him.

"And the servants that Ulmoth suborned, when Astresse and I went against him, not demons?"

"Monsters."

"A distinct word, unrelated in origin," he noted, as though to himself. "So what is a demon, then? What has everyone recognised, in this thing we face?"

"Something from outside." She felt he must be testing her. "Something that is not part of the world, and that wishes us harm."

"Outside," again more to himself than her, and then waved his fingers at the night sky. "Up there?"

"No, *outside*," and she had the curious feeling that now it was *he*, the Elder, failing to understand *her*.

The next morning she was awakened by Allwer's yell. He

had taken the last watch, and the dawn had brought more than just daylight down through the branches.

Lyn had her sword out before she made any decision about it, leaping up and swinging the point at the gaps between the trees. Her dreams had been full of demon-taint anyway, familiar faces and places disfigured by that scaly, eye-pocked growth. Now she expected a staggering host of the merged and the eaten-away, the malformed and the unrecognisable to be emerging all around the clearing.

There was just one visitor, though, and if it was not exactly welcome, nor was it demon touched. Nyrgoth had called down the monstrous flying servant.

The first rays of the dawn touched its metal hide as it swung ponderously towards them through the air. The rings that were its wings, each wide enough that Lyn could have fallen lengthways through them, rattled the branches, sending a fine dust springing away from them. It had lost a leg since last they saw it, and its carapace bore shiny scars from who knew what encounters. It was still a fearsome sight so close, though. Nyrgoth stood before it, one hand up and his fingers seeming to signal and govern its descent. The three of them watched him silently, there in the monster's shadow and yet undaunted. Lyn thought about what he'd said, how the creature was left over from the distant past. It had been a magician's servant, and now it had no master and so it shadowed Nyrgoth, hoping he would instruct it.

He spoke to it in words none of them knew, sometimes commanding, sometimes questioning. It had no voice of its own, but his manner suggested that satisfactory answers came to him somehow, and at last it rose unsteadily into the air, veered abruptly sideways to rip and scrabble against a tree, tearing up the outer layers so that the sap jetted out in a mist, and then returned to the air, ascending until it was only a shape again.

"It will wait on," Nyrgoth said. "There is not much life left in it. Its strength dwindled over the centuries it slept. And I fear what might happen if this infection is capable of touching it. Best it keeps its distance for now."

"But you have a plan," Lyn finished for him, and his face twitched and a very small smile came to it.

"Some thoughts."

"Will it fight the demon for us?"

"Let us first see the demon."

Allwer reckoned they would see Farbourand before the end of the day, even with their slower rate of progress. The forest around them was becoming more infested with the demon-mark, meaning they had to go out of their way to avoid the worst thickets of it. Lyn had expected them to simply meet more and more corruption as they progressed, but the mark was in patches, spread out through the forest. Whole stands of trees were furred over with thick coats of leaf-like scales, glittering with malign scrutiny and bristling with lazily waving feelers. Often there were animals caught within the mesh, no hard division between them and the branches and trunks. Their bodies pulsed and twitched, but then so did the trees themselves. Some gluts of infection were in constant motion, the actual boles of the trees twining about themselves like slow, anxious fingers, the roots rippling to slowly drag whole vast assemblages through the forest, leaving a churned trail of devastation behind them.

One such interconnected knot of trees had a human being within it. They came to it by the screaming. She—Lyn's best guess—was partly within two trunks, as though she had hidden there before the corruption had overtaken her. Now there was only the shape to show that there had been an extra body tucked into the clump of trees. The plants themselves were stretching farther apart, then back together, with a rhythm uncomfortably like breathing, and the human form stretched to bone-popping dimensions with each convulsion. The scream came with the expansion, ripping out of the scale-fringed hole in the otherwise featureless face.

"Just noise," Nyrgoth Elder assured them. "Just the air being forced out of the lungs." She wasn't sure if he was saying so because the alternative was too horrible to consider.

"You can't use your power to save her?" she tried. "Like you did Esha."

"You saw what you had to do, to carve the thing from your friend." Nyrgoth was staring at the screaming thing with that frightening dispassion, that she bitterly coveted in moments like this. "You saw the things that attacked us at Birchari. Can you imagine what would be left, once you cut away all that infected flesh?" He frowned, and leant forward so close to the trees that Lyn feared for him. "I hear the demon's voice," he said. "I hear it in the moment of its arrival like an echo in a cave, but not the original voice of it. It comes from no direction I know. . . ."

"Even as you spoke with your familiar," she pointed out.

Nyrgoth shook his head. "No. That . . . has a very plain explanation, if you but knew the secret to it. But for this I have no explanation. It should be as you say, some similar manipulation of the way the world is, but . . . I can't account for it." And he was more discomforted by that, she could see, than she was. How much worse to think yourself wise, and still be as ignorant as one who knew themselves a fool?

The one blessing was that they saw very few free-moving parts of the demon's army. Those people and beasts still able to move were kept at the edge of the demon's influence, she guessed, where they might march and spread it farther. Here, whatever was left was all warped into one. They were behind enemy lines.

They did not go down to Farbourand. The outpost, the farthest extent of the forest kingdoms' influence, was sheathed entirely in the demon's mark, and within the bowed palisade some huge, single thing rocked and bleated, its bloated, rounded mass visible over the wall, filling almost all the space. They passed on quickly and for once the sorcerer sought no closer study.

Soon after, Allwer stated they were close to the demon's house, and with evening coming they made camp.

"If we make a fire, will it know?" Lyn asked, but Nyrgoth had no answer. He had been quiet all day, sunk into himself. Now he could only say, "I don't know. I can't say anything about this. I don't know why I don't know." And then, just as she was drawing back with the resolution to pass a cold night as best she could, he gripped her wrist.

She froze. *Is it now? Does he demand some price from me, or else he'll leave us here?* He wasn't looking at her, though; the fingers seemed to have acted of their own volition.

"I will need time, tonight," he said awkwardly. "But I cannot just go and find my own camp, away from here. I need to face the enemies that lie within me, like before. And I am afraid, Lyn. Lynesse. Because of what we have seen, and because of my own ignorance. I should be the master of any strangeness in this world, because my people know the secrets of the universe. We travel the night sky and craft objects of power and change our very bodies so that we are no longer heir to the frailties of humanity. And yet I am in this forest with you, and the darkness between the trees is just as fearsome to me." His voice was flat, the affectless tone fighting against the actual words he used.

"What do you need, Elder?" she asked him. "What can I do?" *Here it comes, and I will have no chance but to pay his price.*

But he just said, "I don't know. It wasn't like this with Astresse. I am going to *feel*, Lyn. And it will hurt. And I won't want to go on. I won't want to do anything. And if it gets very bad, I may just want to die. And I can only tell you these things because my protections hold. I can be so very dispassionate about these things, right now. But the reckoning has come. I can't hide from it, and I will need to think clearly tomorrow."

Lyn thought about feeling, the good and the bad of it. "We will have no fire tonight," she said, "but we can have the things the firelight brings, when friends are together in a hard place. And perhaps that will help you feel other things, better things."

He stared at her blankly, and she went to talk to the others.

Later, she saw the moment that he withdrew his iron control: no grand outburst, no railing at the sky, just an inwards hunching to him, a sagging of his head. He was doing his very best to hide it, she realised, because shame is a feeling, too. So, when she spoke, it was not to him but to Esha and Allwer, and what she told was a story.

Lyn had grown up on stories. She was in this mess, this self-appointed duty on her shoulders, precisely because of them. When a thing like this demon arose, a princess of the blood should step forth to combat it. That was how the world was supposed to be. And so she told such a story, some princess of the dawn age, some other threat, met with steel and bold words and a defiant spirit. She made the best performance of it she could, remembering how such tellings had made her feel, sitting at her mother's knee back when she was too young to know any better.

Esha took over then, giving them one of the Coast-people's twisting story-in-story-in-stories, full of humiliation for the proud and fortune for the clever. Allwer had what looked to be a story about three brothers at first, but then turned into a spectacularly ribald joke that nobody back home would ever have dared tell a Fourth Daughter. Then it was Lyn's turn again, and she conjured up another tale of heroes, some time-smudged past era when another demon had come from *outside* to be faced with courage and blades and the solving of riddles. And so it went, around the circle where the fire should be, and Lyn stole glances at the huddled sorcerer and tried to work out if any of this was having the desired effect. He did not laugh at the joke or at the funny turns in Esha's tale. He did not seem to rally at her own inspirational hero-talk. And yet she could tell that he listened.

And then, when her turn came about for the third time, she summoned her courage to reach over and touch him on the arm, cocking her head in invitation.

"Very well then." His voice was slow and bleak, but all the stories had hooked something deep inside him and hauled it up to the air, nonetheless. "I will tell the story of a sorcerer."

He had told her many things before, that he had plainly expected her not to understand, but which had been entirely transparent to her. Talk of the ancients, of magical workers and familiar spirits, all of it fitting neatly with her own tales and what she knew about the world. This story of his was not like that. She could not follow it, and he told it poorly because to be a magician was not the same thing as being a bard, and who did he have, in his tower, to practice the craft on? He went back on himself or repeated himself, corrections and contradictions and leaps in logic that nobody could quite follow him in. And yet the sense of it came over: there was a sorcerer, but the sorcerer was just a man. He had travelled from the otherworld of the sorcerers, which was the world her ancestors had journeyed from, long ago. He had come to his tower—his outpost, as he called it—to watch and study, and not interfere. But then the other ancients had left and returned to their otherworld and closed its doors behind them, and he ceased to hear their voices through the night sky, and he feared that all his kind, every one of them, had met some dark fate. The craft of travelling the rivers of the sky was lost, many mortal lifetimes ago. He was the last.

And she'd known he was the last of the Elders, but she had never stopped to think what that *meant*. How terrible it was to know yourself the last of anything.

But, at the end of the telling, something of the burden was gone from him. The set of his body said that the beast still loomed over him, but perhaps it had been driven off a pace or two. Lyn took his hand, and then Esha his other one, and after an awkward moment Allwer made up the circle.

"Tell me of Astresse and Ulmoth," Nyrgoth said, almost like a child at bedtime. "Tell it to me, the way you know it. Tell me how we were."

And so Lyn found one last tale within her, and gave the full rendition of the deeds of her glorious ancestor, and told the sorcerer how he was remembered: Nyrgoth Elder, terrible, wise and mighty, whose magic had turned Ulmoth's behemoths of destruction to mere statues so that Astresse could meet the warlord blade on blade and slay him.

At the end, he was smiling, and weeping also. "It wasn't like that," he said. "Not really. But your way is better. Keep telling it like that." And then, after a long time staring at her, "You are not Astresse."

She flinched, but he hadn't meant it as a criticism.

"I must remember that. You are so like her, but you are not her." And then, when she thought he'd said his piece, "I loved her as much as I have ever loved anything. Which is not so very much. And you are not her, but for our compact I will destroy the demon for you if I can."

Nyr

WE ARE WITHIN AN hour's walk of the demon's house, by Allwer's reckoning. It's time for me to earn my keep as wizard, I suppose.

I activate my drone, first of all: the insect-sized thing doesn't have the power for prolonged operations, but I'm intending to run this whole business remotely and it will have to be my eyes. Based on the satellite map and Allwer's testimony, I guide it to where the demon lives, wondering what I'll see.

Not a house. Beyond that I hit the realm of guesswork almost immediately.

The actual spread of infection here is surprisingly localised, no more than half a kilometre across, thinnest at the edges, then making a dense and riotous ring of growth about midway in, and then flattening out towards the centre again. But then I've already worked out that the "demon" is not about holding ground for territory's sake.

In the centre there is something that the drone's inadequate sensors say might be a crash site, or might be some

other form of intrusion. The ground is rippled and dis-
torted, and at its heart something has grown. This isn't
just some pre-existing structure layered over with the
growth we have seen elsewhere. This is a novel eruption,
a battery of twining tendrils or cables, thicker about than
a human body, knotted and tangled around one another
in a way that my mind insists is not random, though no
rational pattern can be seen. The whole visceral assem-
blage arcs out and up and back to a height of perhaps
ten metres or so, where it meets its opposite number and
meshes with it in an ugly, knotted lump, the capstone to
the arch thus formed. And I am making my analysis as
clinical and calm as possible, and leaning heavily on my
DCS, because the arch is a door to somewhere else. It is
not the demon's house, but its gate.

The inadequate senses of the drone do not, I suspect,
do the sight justice. It cannot process what there is to see,
within the confines of the arch. I think there is a landscape through there, but I cannot analyse it in terms of
perspective and distance. I feel that I am trying to process
something not intended to be trapped in the customary
number of dimensions. The drone has given colours to
the view, and though the colours are horrible and clash,
they are also merely artificial labels because it cannot reproduce what it is seeing. I can make nothing of it.

And yet this is the source of the signal. Every pulse resonates through the arch so that the drone picks it up. And yet, draw the drone back a little and there is nothing; the signal itself does not travel out through any detectable space. I can see it sent there, received here, but to make the journey it slips through some void that does not exist for me, and should not exist at all.

The demon is not interested in claiming territory with its mark. Its spires and twisted corpses and other infestations are relays. They are the surfacing points for the signal that enters the world through this door, like a seal rising to a hole in the ice for air, before ducking under once more. And that terrifies me because nowhere in all the science I ever knew did we ever think there was anything under the ice, and now there is a boundless dark sea down there, and things dwell in it.

And I do not know what they want. As I told Lynesse, my brief interrogation revealed no lust to devour, no malice, not even a mere need to reproduce, and yet a definite drive. Less comprehensible in viewpoint than a virus.

The demon's influence, to whatever alien end, is spreading as it intrudes into the world at point after point, but it all springs from this door. There is a physical anchor here that it is dependent on. I must focus on what I can understand.

I call the worker robot. It is a poor tool, leaking battery life and in a wretched state. Now I have asserted authority over it, though, it is desperate to help, following the tattered ends of its original programming. It bombards me with demands for a job queue. I only have the one job, and it would forget anything more anyway.

To Lyn and the others, I am just sitting down, resting my eyes. They hear the worker as it clatters overhead, trailing its broken limbs and shuddering in the air when its repulsor fields falter. But there's still just enough life in the robot for what I need.

It is a construction unit. It has a nice set of diamond teeth. And, if all else fails, I'll blow the battery and hope the explosion will do the job.

I have to rely on my drone, because the robot's own sensor feed is corrupted. I send it in, recklessly fast, so that it almost vanishes into the great anomaly that is the portal itself. Instead, it ends up clinging to the frame with its three working legs.

Sample with extreme prejudice, I instruct it, and its drilling mandibles whirr to life, sheeting dust and rust, dipping towards the arch.

My thinking is based on the conduct of the entity so far—if "entity" is even the correct word. Admittedly it did tear me a new bodily orifice, but other than that our progress through the trees has been uncontested. It has no free-moving parts patrolling the interior; everything it has touched seems to have ended up as part of its relay structures, spreading the signal—which may itself *be* the demon, a thing of no physical substance but that can cause catastrophic changes in living matter. I am proceeding on the basis that, now my field has isolated us from its influence, we do not exist to it.

The worker robot has a very temporary field of a similar nature, created by overclocking its remaining components quite severely. It is the perfect assassin. I have it begin dismantling the fibrous substance of the arch.

I have a certain amount of science behind this, and beyond that I have what Lyn said, about the nature of demons. The science is that my drone's instruments detect a great deal of warped electromagnetic activity about the arch, and even its sensors show that all the usual components of the energy spectrum are being affected as though the arch itself had a gravitational footprint that it, frankly, does not. The impression is of something being unnaturally held into shape by pressure exerted along an axis I cannot perceive. Sever the arch, and where does the space it constrains go? It ceases to be, and my theory is that the signal, the demon, the infection, however I salve my credulity, will cease along with it.

I don't get to test the theory. The moment the robot's teeth bite, the arch comes alive. Spiny tendrils rip free of its corded substance and lash convulsively against the worker robot, hurling it away to bounce and rattle across the scaly ground. It ends up on its back before its flight units hurl it ten feet into the air, so that it comes down tilted against a bristling rise of corrupted spirals that might have been trees once. I get a battery of aggrieved damage reports and then nothing.

With the DCS up, I don't feel the rage that stabs through me, though I can track its footsteps through my readouts. Something obviously gets to my face, though, because Lyn nods flatly.

"It failed."

"Yes," I admit. "The arch attacked it. I need to think of something else."

"Do you have something else?" She seems as calm as I am, and that worries me.

"No. Not yet."

"No words to command it?"

"It's not like . . ." I give up. "Demons are from outside, as you said. They don't respect my words."

"And your familiar?" She gestures at the sky.

"It will spy for us but not act. Not its job."

And she nods. It's devastating, that nod. Or I recognise it would be, if I were allowing myself to be devastated right now. Lynesse Fourth Daughter, who came to the wizard's tower because she needed to fight a demon, finally understands. Not *Your sorcery wasn't strong enough* but the far truer revelation, *You have run out of toys*. I've been telling her all along there's no such thing as magic. Now I see she believes me, and I find that I was relying on her belief in magic because I'm all out of other options and magic was probably the only thing that might have beaten the odds and come through for us.

"Then there's just one thing for it," she tells us all.

"No," Esha says flatly, though Allwer is nodding slowly.

"These things are solved by two things: a strong arm and a keen blade. That is how the tales have it. There is no other way." And I can see that, despite the admirable confidence in her voice, she is scared to death. "I will step through the door of the demon's house and slay it. I alone. I will not ask it of any of you."

Allwer is plainly not volunteering, and in the end Esha can just shake her head and back off. And as for me . . .

"There must be another way," I tell her. "You cannot go through that gate. Whatever lies beyond, it is inimical to human life, even to physical matter as we know it. You would be unmade, and your sword as well. This is suicide." And I see her rebuttal even as she opens her mouth to speak it. "Give me time, please. Let me find how I can dismantle this thing, turn it off, break it apart. Enough energy, enough force . . ." But if the robot failed, what can I do? Lyn is about to turn me down and so I draw myself up to my full height, so much taller than any of them.

I drag together the full mummery she has invested me with and say, "Why did you come to my tower, if not to use my magic against the demon?"

"Magic," she echoes.

I force myself to nod. Am I not a wizard, however I try to express it?

At last, she inclines her head. "Sunrise," she says at last. "Next sunrise, and I will go. If you have no magic to defeat the demon by then, it will be arm and sword, and no more."

———————

I do not sleep. No great hardship compared to all the other things I'm staving off. I do not want Lynesse Fourth Daughter to go through that door. I do not believe in her stories or that this thing can be bested with any number of strong arms or swords. It's ridiculous, isn't it? Primitive, savage beliefs in a people who once walked the stars.

And yet I pore over the data received from my drone and from the doomed worker robot, and in the end I have no answers to the big question. They call it a demon, and I have no better term to offer. It does what it does in defiance of any scientific understanding. I can see only the effects of its presence, not the means by which it accomplishes them. How can it coordinate its parts without its signals passing through the intervening space? How does it manifest its mark, a profusion of semi-organic growth that does not have anywhere to draw sufficient mass from? Nothing about it makes sense. And I, whose power over the world resides in my knowledge of its workings, am therefore impotent.

Or not quite impotent. If the arch can be destroyed . . . But if Lyn takes an edge to it, she'll fare no better than the robot.

We are still two hours off dawn, by my internal clock, when I have the answer. Not my first choice, to be honest. Dire enough that I don't want to do it, actually. A really stupid idea, from the point of view of Nyr Illim Tevitch, scientist. For Nyrgoth Elder, some-sort-of-wizard-apparently, it seems almost fitting. Mythic, you might say.

I am going to make a momentous decision. Most likely it is a bad decision. Certainly it may be the last major decision I ever make. A terrible, bleak decision born of despair, surely. The decision only a man overcome by the beast that hunts him would make.

And for that reason I throw my DCS into high gear, banish every scrap of misery, love and hate, all the emotional baggage. Back to your oubliette. Grown-ups are talking.

With that artificial and antiseptic clarity I consider exactly what I am going to do, clinical as a computer. I expect the whole plan to evaporate in that harsh light. To turn out to be no more than bad ideas born of bad thoughts and self-loathing. Yet the shocking thing is (or would be, could I be shocked) that it all holds up. The chain of logic, the lack of other options. If I want this end, then I require these means. And the lack of affect I'm working under means that the usual human rejection of such dire measures doesn't come either. *Yes,* my absolutely clear mind tells me. *This is a workable plan.* At this late hour, both sides of my nature reach across the border and shake hands on it. *This is the only recourse now.*

I need to tell her face-to-face, and that means I drop the DCS and let all the emotion back in. That is how it should be. I need my voice to tremble, when I explain the plan to her. I need her to see in my face just how serious I am about this. Most of all I need to *feel.* I cannot propose such a measure as this as though it's like filling in a necessary but onerous form.

And yet, when I confront her in the morning, and she already garbed for war, buckling on her sword belt, all I can do is stare at her. Gaze at her. She is so like Astresse, and Astresse would never have gone along with something like my plan. And neither will Lyn.

I can feel the tears pricking at my eyes. Worse, I can

feel the absolute assurance that this won't work, that I won't be able to talk her out of her stupid plan and into mine, which will seem so much worse to her. Which *is* so much worse, because most likely it means we'll both die, rather than just her. I just stand there before her expectant gaze and say nothing, and then say nothing some more, until the only thing I can do is bring the DCS back online. Sometimes you can't get things done, with all that in the way. Sometimes sincerity has to take a back seat.

"Let us walk," I tell her. "I will go with you." I say nothing about the plan, not yet. That turns out to be the logical decision.

Lynesse

ESHA DIDN'T WANT TO let her go, but wanted even less to go into the heart of the demon's realm. In the end Lyn had to pull together all her authority as princess of Lannesite. "Someone must tell my mother," she insisted. "When you have seen how things fall out. And you," to Allwer. "You were not always a good man, but you have been a good man in this. You have earned your reprieve."

After that, there was no more to it than to go, not even a long trek, save that they would be passing through forest utterly conquered by the demon. They had to wind their way, finding paths broad enough to admit them and, even then, the bushy growth of scale that encrusted every surface quivered and reached for them as they passed, extruding whip-like feelers that got within inches of their skin before recoiling from the invisible shield the sorcerer had about them.

Some of what they passed through had likely been more than just trees. The lopsided, furred-over shapes were suggestive of other bodies. The dense profusion of the demon-mark became a blessing, hiding what it had grown upon.

Nyrgoth Elder was very quiet at Lyn's side, walking with long, solemn strides and head downcast.

"You think I'm going to die," she accused him, although she might as well have been speaking to her own mind, which had not let up on the subject since they set out.

He stopped, staring at nothing, or inwards. "When we reach the gate," he said, then faltered, closing his eyes and summoning his resolve. "When we reach the gate," he repeated, "you must do as I ask you. Will you swear to it? You may not want to." And then a brief twist of a smile. "Or perhaps you will. Who knows? But do it. Swear to it. As a hero or a princess or whatever is appropriate."

"What is it?"

"Wizardly things. Oaths and words of great power. Magic," he said.

"Magic is just the secret ways of the world. Tell me."

He tried to. She saw the will to do so rise up within him, but find no way to the outside world. "I have lived a long time," he said at last. "Ridiculously long. And to no purpose."

In such a way he managed to communicate his meaning to her, without ever having to say the words.

And then, without warning, they had broken out into

the central bowl of the demon's domain, and were before the arch.

Nyrgoth had tried to describe it, but there were no words that might have prepared her for the sight. She felt her stomach knot with vertigo, staring through the arch at whatever lay beyond. It was bright, lurid. She had no names for any of the colours and they hurt her eyes. Parts of her mind threw up cascades of chaotic thoughts and images, just to look upon it. She thought she saw distant peaks and chasms, umbral and vast. A moment later they were no more than the wrinkles on skin held too close to the eye. The hideous distortion of it weighed down the world so that everything sloped inwards towards the arch. At the same time it seemed higher, lifted aloft, so that to approach would be to climb a barbed slope. There was no sound in the clearing, and despite that she could hear the world screaming at the wound opened into its substance. The air stank of rotting tin and soured gold.

She drew her sword, feeling only a great weight of hopelessness. Nyrgoth had told her this could not be ended with a blade and now she saw he was right. But a blade was all she had.

She took three steps towards the arch, fighting the world and herself for each one. "I will do this," she swore. "I am Lynesse Fourth Daughter. I am my mother's disappointment and my sisters' mockery, and I have no purpose but this. I will save the world. Come out and fight me, demon!"

A squeal of abused metal startled her. The wizard's monstrous servant, which had been lying unnoticed on its side, abruptly rocked and shuddered, remaining legs moving weakly. Nyrgoth was staring at it thoughtfully.

"Is that your plan? To send your monster in again?" she demanded, hearing her voice tremble.

"No, but..." Nyrgoth looked about them sharply. "Ah."

"Ah?" Even as she echoed him, she understood. There was a slow rippling undulation passing through the surrounding growth, scales flexing and standing on end in sequence, a flurry of little tendrils chasing across the mottled surface. The pinhead beads of eyes moved and merged, becoming greater orbs: size of a fist, size of a head, until there were great dark wells staring out at them from all sides.

"It knows we're here," she understood.

"It has detected something, even if just the absence of itself in our shadow. I hear it interrogating me again. We have very limited time." Nyrgoth took a deep breath. "I said you couldn't do this with a blade."

"You did, yes."

"I was wrong." There were odd muscles twitching about his face, and she realised with fascinated horror that she was seeing the real man, the bitterly unhappy victim of his own mind, trying to make himself known. What would that man say to her? Not to listen to the calm words his lips were telling her. "Lynesse Fourth Daughter, now is the time to do exactly as I say, and no more or less." And he was fumbling with his clothing, to her incredulous horror. He was fiddling with the bindings and fastenings, that were all in the wrong place, until at last he had them free and had pulled back his robe and tunic and shift, shrugging them off his shoulders to reveal a lean chest and soft stomach. All around them the demon-marked mounds were shifting and swaying, and parts of them seemed to be bulging up as though the tangled mass was trying to give up the forms of animals and people. She saw a brief suggestion of limbs, of faces, and looked away hurriedly, meeting Nyrgoth's eyes.

"You must do it," he told her. "I can't do it myself. Not even with the pain hidden away from me. I lack that kind of courage." In three steps he was before the arch, watching the hungry feelers and barbed vines rise up from it like serpents, questing curiously through the air. Nyrgoth turned back to her, arms out. "Take your steel. Cut here." The place he marked was beneath his ribs, close to where the demon's servant had gutted him. She could just see the pale line of the wound, as though it had happened a generation ago. "Cut, and what you unleash shall undo the demon, if anything can. But be swift."

"I don't know if I can," she whispered, but she had her blade out, tip scratching a bead of blood from his belly. There were stories, of course: one hero of the ancients had to unseam the Firebird that had carried them across the night, to release all the good things of the world that it had swallowed. Another had gone across the world cutting apart scattered seeds of the Tree of Changes to birth the first Coast-people. Stories, myths, contradictory parables. True without being real. But this was real.

"Lyn," he said, "I have been without purpose for a long time. At least let me be useful to your world in this way."

"Tell it to me without your shield. Tell it to me in your real voice, with your real self behind it," she challenged him. She was having difficulty keeping the sword steady, her own hands were shaking so much.

"This is me, all of me." Behind her the metal servant righted itself abruptly with a tremendous rattle of loose plates, and she twitched and drove the blade two inches into his gut. His face went white, but somehow he conjured a smile.

"Yes. But all at once, please. There's a limit to how much I can hold back the pain and still function." He reached out with his fingertips and touched her hand, clenched about the weapon's hilt. "Lyn . . ."

She lunged, driving the weapon into him and then

drawing it out with a twist to free it from his flesh, as she'd been taught. He made a soft sound, almost of revelation. Then she had staggered back two steps, feeling the crawling horror of the demon clutching for her from behind, the horror of what she had done from the front.

Nyrgoth reached with crooked fingers, driving them stiffly into the wound, clawing into his own body and fumbling there, teeth gritted, eyes clenched shut. Then, with a great cry, he tore something free, that was the size of Lyn's fist and ragged with gore.

"Lie there, no matter what happens to my body," he got out, and dropped the bloody trophy before the arch, and then howled at the sky, at the demon, at the world, "Do it now! *Now!*"

He dropped to his knees and she was rushing to catch him, feeling his long, awkward body slump into her, shivering and twitching. All around her there were things breaking away from the demon's massed corruption, shapes part-human, part-beast, merged, blended, clumsy on too many limbs or too few. She lifted her red sword and resolved to make them pay dearly for her last moments.

Then the servant, the worker, had lurched over to her, almost knocking her down. She struck at it with her sword, carving a bright scar on its metal hide, but it just stood there, whining and whirring. Incredibly, Nyrgoth pawed at it, painting it with his blood. His lips moved, and she read one word there.

On.

He tried to fight her, when she hauled him up. That might have been because he wanted her to leave him; it might have been because the pain had broken through his barriers so that being bodily dragged over the back of his servant was agony to him. She had no time for niceties. By the time she was astride the creature herself, she didn't know if he was alive or dead.

"Whatever you're going to do," she told the thing, "do it now."

She almost fell off, when it lumbered into the air, every metal part of it protesting and its innards roaring as though it shared all its master's pain. She clung to it and to Nyrgoth's body, watching the eye-twisting arch recede, watching long flailing tentacles thrash from the demonic overgrowth to reach for her, then fall back down like cut ropes. The servant carried them away, shuddering through the sky, losing height abruptly with stomach-lurching drops, then clambering skywards again, listing perilously to one side.

Behind her, the world turned to light and fire.

Lynesse

BACK HOME AT HER mother's court, of course, nobody believed a word of it.

It would have been worse if Esha and Allwer had not turned up. Lyn knew exactly how much worse, because they were long days behind her. They had not been carried part of the way by a flying monster. Not that anyone believed that either. For those days before Esha knelt before the throne of Lannesite and told her story, Lyn felt the full lash of her mother's bitter disappointment. Not a new vintage, you'd have thought, save that this was the final straw, the very last act of her least dutiful daughter. And when Lyn had recalled their ancestor Astresse Once Regent and her bargain with the Elder sorcerer, her mother had just shaken her head and castigated her for squandering such a resource at the whim of a foolish girl. As far as her mother was concerned, Lyn was just a grown woman who had not put away her childish toys. The world was built on trade agreements and intelligence reports and what the next harvest season would bring. Stories of heroes and demons were for the fire, for drunken nights, for children.

Then Esha arrived at Lannesite, breathless, using up all her own credit at court for an urgent audience with the queen. She explained what they had seen under the demon's aegis—no more than Lyn had seen, but Esha Free Mark was a marginally more reliable witness.

She had seen the fire from heaven. She had seen Lyn descend, riding the monster and with the sorcerer's body slung before her like a trophy. She'd seen more than Lyn had, then. Lyn had been inconsolable, weeping, seeing only that corpse. Esha had, instead, watched the world around them.

She told how the demon's mark had begun flaking off everything it clung to, the scales blowing away like dead leaves and turning to rust, the little black eyes cracking and shrivelling. What was left beneath, when that covering was thrown back, had not been pretty. The trees and beasts and people of the Ordwood had been eaten away, blended, recombined in experimental ways as though by some mind that had no idea quite what they were or how they worked. Esha and Allwer could confirm every trace of the demon was disintegrating.

Which had left Nyrgoth Elder.

They had no way to help him. He seemed dead, but perhaps "dead" meant something different. Perhaps it meant something less permanent. If they only could . . .

Lyn had been shouting and screaming at the mute monster, demanding it help. Demanding it take the wizard's body back to his tower, where his magic was strongest. It ignored her. It only spoke Wizard, Esha guessed. They knew the Elder had his own speech. Why would his familiar respond to the words of regular people?

And nobody spoke Wizard, of course, but Esha did speak every other language known within two hundred miles. All the trade speech and the guild speech, all the tangle of related cants and dialects that people had carried to every corner of the world. More, whenever the wizard had spoken in his own way, to himself or to the monster, she had listened just as she'd listen to any traveller from a distant land. So Esha catechised the monster with every manner of speech she knew, hunting out any words they had in common. Because she knew there were some words that were close as sisters in all languages. Basic words, fundamentally human words. Words even a monster might know. "Mother." "Father." Such a basic concept, and there were only a handful of ways to say it, in thirty different languages.

And something she said reached it. Some word so fundamental that humans and wizards alike shared it. "Home." And the monster had been airborne again, carrying Lyn and Nyrgoth's corpse, with her friends left behind. Which was why Lyn arrived at court long before them.

For Lyn, Esha's arrival meant some slight lessening of her mother's disregard, to find that her Fourth Daughter had not just been wandering starry-eyed through the forests fighting with sticks. And yet, as though something of the demon clung to her, too deep rooted to dig out, catharsis never came. Her mother never stopped scowling. As though defeating the demon and saving the Ordwood meant nothing. Lannesite didn't really care about the Ordwood, Lyn realised. Or perhaps a weaker and more divided Ordwood might be preferable. Even with Esha's testimony, she could see everyone still doubted the details. Esha had lost her edge years before, after all, and Allwer was no more than a criminal. Something had happened, and now it had stopped happening, but was it really plausible that Lynesse had a hand in any of it? Lynesse the simpleton, the dreamer?

In her chambers, barred from her mother's presence, she clung to what she could. She had defeated the demon, whatever they believed. She had ridden the familiar monster all the way to its home, the tower. And there she had hauled the elder's body to the door and yelled at it until its invisible guardian had opened it for her. Then she'd yelled at the empty interior that she'd brought its master back for burial, by whatever traditions sorcerers held to.

When at last it had opened a panel in the wall, revealing a coffin-space within, she had done the last part of her duty. Interred the last of the Elders in his place of power. Spoken some words. And left.

———————

Nineteen days after Esha's return, a messenger appeared at the palace, a woman whose voice shook as she recounted her missive. A monster had appeared to her, she said: a flying thing with a hide of metal and teeth of crystal. It had hung in the sky above her and spoken with a stone's voice, calling that Lynesse Fourth Daughter come to the sorcerer's tower, and that she bring Esha Free Mark and Allwer Once Exile with her, by the invitation of Nyrgoth Elder.

And Lyn had the profound satisfaction of standing before her mother and the whole court and saying, "Well?"

Nyr

THE SATELLITE ISN'T TALKING to me anymore.

I don't know exactly if this is because, once it exercised the Ultimate Anti-contamination Measures, I just don't exist to it anymore. After all, as far as it's concerned, it's just obliterated my body to stop the locals getting hold of it and all the precious technology it contains.

On the other hand, it might be the locator. It wasn't my heart I actually ripped from my own chest, after all, but it was my beacon, that let the satellite know exactly where I was. I was right there, where the gateway stood, as far as it was concerned. And now I'm not *here*, because I don't have a beacon anymore, so the satellite ignores my requests to link with it. My familiar spirit has been cut from me.

And if my Explorer Corps colleagues return, somehow, after so long, if Earth signals me or sends a ship to bring me home, I won't know, and the satellite will tell them I am dead. And probably tell them I was a very poor anthropologist, even for second class. And the first might be false, but the second will very definitely be true.

I thought the worker robot would get Lyn out. When I linked to it and found it had rebooted itself, I gave it that command. And somehow it came back here and Lyn told the outpost to admit her, and it did. I have gone back over the records. It's when she basically hauls my unre-sisting body upright and leans me against the door, like some kind of grisly farce, that my blood chemistry gets recognised by the outpost systems and it opens up. Then she just shouts at the walls and eventually the tower sys-tems work out what the situation is and put out a healing capsule, and Lyn bodily rolls me into it.

When the clear lid comes down and it retracts, with me inside, she sits with her back to the wall and weeps. I don't think it's for me, exactly, just a release of all that pent-up grief and anger and sheer soured adrenaline. Just a lot inside her to get out, and of all people I can certainly understand that.

Eventually, of course, she goes home.

Somewhat more eventually, the outpost wakes me up, and I sort through the torrid history of tolerance warnings and medical tuttings until I concede that I am still alive and functional and totally isolated from the wider universe. I send a long-range drone west, and the next time I let the DCS down I hope that some part of the cocktail of emotion that assails me is a profound satisfaction that the plan worked. The land the demon took will not be well for a long time, a great blighted scar across the Ordwood, and in the minds of its people. Whatever the demon was, though, it is gone, the signal cut off where it entered our . . . world? Universe? Reality? I cannot guess.

And by then it's time for me to flush out my mind without the benefit of the DCS, and it's still bad, all that pent-up negative stuff. Just because I did good doesn't mean I don't feel bad, because the feeling bad, it's not particularly *because* of anything that's happened; it's just the way I'm wired. But in the midst of it I think about Lyn and Esha and Allwer and the whole mad business, and I can smile a bit, and think, *Those days, eh?* Just as I did with Astresse and Ulmoth.

And I should go back to sleep, really, to wait for . . . what, though?

When Ulmoth was defeated, I remember parting from Astresse. I would return to my outpost, to wait for my colleagues and my people and word from distant Earth. But she could call on me, of course. If she had need, or if her line had need, Nyrgoth Elder would be there for them. Nyr, as she called me. And that was as far as I was willing to bend the rules, and it was an unforgivable breach anyway. Staying with her would have been a step too far. And now . . .

She's dead these hundred years. And while she lived,

she never did quite need me enough to come to the outpost and wake me. I made that promise to her bloodline, and she took me at my word, very seriously indeed, when actually I had been asking her to come back for me, to save me from myself.

Or else, once she was immersed in the running of the kingdom, her adventure with the sorcerer had gone from memory to myth inside her mind, and eventually she put away childish things.

And where does that leave me, now?

I repair the robot, or enough for one more flight, and send it to deliver a message. And then I wait.

———————

Later, after they arrive, I watch Allwer regrowing his lost fingers and hope I can store up the joy for later use, and that it won't just sour into dismay as these things so often do. And I stand with Lyn and look out of the outpost's eyes at the entourage her mother gave her, to come here. Not just two ragged travellers this time: an honour guard and courtiers who are also spies for the Crown, tents, flunkies, riding animals, all that. And I force them to stay outside and camp in the hard places because I can be petty like that. Only Lyn, Esha, and Allwer get to come in. My companions, the demon-slayers.

And I decide, with my most rational mind, that I am no longer an anthropologist. My failures of objectivity and detachment surely mean that anything I wrote would be hopelessly contaminated by my involvement with the culture I purport to study. Similarly, this place is no longer an outpost. To be an outpost requires some larger thing to be posted out of, and I can be honest with myself: there is no larger thing; not for any practical intents and purposes, and most likely not at all in any way. This is nothing but a tower, and I am nothing but a scientist of sufficiently advanced technology, which is to say a magician.

"I was thinking that I might come to court with you," I say idly to Lyn. Live a life amongst her people, tell stories that seem one way for me, but which my listeners will forever hear in some other way denied me. Be the court magician of Lannesite. And grow old, I do not say. And, at last, give up my absurdly attenuated existence, I also omit. But first, I will have lived.

In Lyn's eyes I see a spark. Not for me, Nyr Illim Tevitch, but for a world where there are sorcerers and monsters and wonders, and where courage and resolve can solve problems that intrigue and bookkeeping cannot. The last age of magic, perhaps.

Or perhaps not. The tower will still stand. Its systems will last for half a millennium, a hundred Storm-seasons and more. And if I am to be a wizard, maybe I should take on an apprentice.

Lyn grins at me, and I lift the cognitive shielding, and for a moment I am happy.

Acknowledgments

Thank you to my agent, Simon Kavanagh; my editor, Lee Harris; everyone else involved at Tordotcom; and Liz Myles for acting as an advance reader.

About the Author

© Kate Eshelby

ADRIAN TCHAIKOVSKY is the author of the acclaimed Shadows of the Apt fantasy series and the epic science fiction blockbuster *Children of Time*. He has won the Arthur C. Clarke Award, a British Fantasy Award, and a British Science Fiction Association Award, and been nominated for the David Gemmell Legend Award and the Brave New Words Award. In civilian life he is a gamer and amateur entomologist. He was a full-time lawyer until recently, when he decided to write full-time instead.

TOR·COM

Science fiction. Fantasy. The universe.

And related subjects.

*

More than just a publisher's website, *Tor.com*
is a venue for **original fiction, comics,** and
discussion of the entire field of SF and fantasy,
in all media and from all sources. Visit our site
today—and join the conversation yourself.